VOWS MADE
IN SECRET

VOWS MADE IN SECRET

BY

LOUISE FULLER

First published in Great Britain 2015
by Mills & Boon, an imprint of Harlequin (UK) Limited,
Large Print edition 2015
Eton House, 18-24 Paradise Road,
Richmond, Surrey, TW9 1SR

© 2015 Louise Fuller

ISBN: 978-0-263-25697-0

Printed and bound in Great Britain
by CPI Antony Rowe, Chippenham, Wiltshire

To my husband, Patrick,
who provided inspiration not just for
the love scenes but the emotional conflict!

CHAPTER ONE

SCOWLING, A LOCK of dark hair falling onto his forehead, Laszlo Cziffra de Zsadany stared at the young woman with smooth fair hair. His jaw tightened involuntarily as he studied her face in silence, noting the contrast between the innocence of the soft grey eyes and the passionate promise of her full mouth.

She was beautiful. So beautiful that it was impossible not to stand and stare. Such beauty could seduce and enslave. For such a woman a man would relinquish his throne, betray his country and lose his sanity.

Laszlo smiled grimly. He might even get married!

His smile faded and, feeling restless and on edge, he leant forward and squinted at the cramped, curled inscription at the bottom of the painting. Katalina Csesnek de Veszprem. But even though his eyes were fixed intently on the writing his mind kept drifting back to the face of the sitter. He gritted his teeth. What was it about this painting that he found so unsettling? But even as he asked himself the question he shrank from acknowledging the answer.

Anger jostled with misery as he stared at the face, seeing not Katalina but another, whose name was never spoken for to do so would burn his lips. Of course it wasn't so very like *her*; there were similarities, in colouring and the shape of her jaw, but that was all.

Disconcerted by the intense and unwelcome emotions stirred up by a pair of grey eyes, he glanced longingly out of the window at the Hungarian countryside. And then he froze as he heard an unmistakable hooting. It was bad luck to hear an owl's cry in daylight and his golden eyes narrowed as he uneasily searched the pale blue sky for the bird.

From behind him there was a thump as Besnik, his lurcher, sat down heavily on the stone floor. Sighing, Laszlo reached down and rubbed the dog's silky ears between his thumb and forefinger.

'I know,' he murmured softly. 'You're right. I need some air. Come.' Standing up straight, he clicked his fingers so that the dog leapt lightly to its feet. 'Let's go! Before I start counting magpies.'

He wandered slowly through the castle's corridors. The wood panelling on the walls gleamed under the low lights, and the familiar smell of beeswax and lavender calmed him as he walked down the stairs. Passing his grandfather's study, he noticed that the door was ajar and, glancing inside, he saw with some surprise that the room wasn't empty; his grandfather, Janos, was sitting at his desk.

Laszlo felt his chest tighten as he took in how small and frail Janos appeared to be. Even now, more than six years after his wife Annuska's death, his grandfather still seemed to bear the burden of her loss. For a moment he hesitated. And then, softly, he closed the door. There had been an almost meditative quality to his grandfather's stillness and he sensed that Janos needed to be alone.

He wondered why his grandfather was up so early. And then he remembered. Of course. Seymour was arriving today!

No wonder Janos had been unable to sleep. Collecting art had been his hobby for over thirty years: a personal, private obsession. But today, for the first time ever, he would reveal that collection to a stranger—this expert, Edmund Seymour, who was arriving from London.

Laszlo grimaced. He instinctively distrusted

strangers and he felt a ripple of dislike for Seymour—a man he'd never met, and to whom he had never so much as uttered a word, but whose company he would now have to suffer for weeks.

Pushing a door open with his shoulder, he glanced warily into the kitchen and then breathed out slowly. Good! Rosa wasn't up. He wasn't ready to face her gimlet eye yet. Apart from his grandfather their housekeeper was the only other person from whom he couldn't hide his feelings. Only, unlike Janos, Rosa had no qualms about cross-examining him.

Pulling open the cavernous fridge, he groaned as he saw the cold meats and salads arranged on the shelves.

And then, despite the rush of cold air on his face, and the even colder lump of resentment in his chest, he felt his mood shift and he closed the fridge door gently. Food had been a comforting distraction during his grandmother's long illness. But by the time of her death it had become a passion—a passion that had led to him financing a restaurant in the centre of Budapest. The restaurant had been his project: it had been a risk, and a lot of hard work, but he thrived on both and he was now the owner of a staggeringly successful chain of high street restaurants.

Laszlo lifted his chin. He was no longer just Janos's grandson but a wealthy, independent businessman in his own right.

He sighed. Not that he wasn't proud of being a de Zsadany. It was just that the name brought certain responsibilities along with it. Such as Seymour's impending visit. He gritted his teeth. If only the blasted man would ring and cancel.

As if on cue, his mobile phone vibrated in his pocket. Clumsy with shock, and a ridiculous sense of guilt, he pulled it out with shaking fingers: it was Jakob! Relief, and the tiniest feeling of regret, washed over him.

'Laszlo! I thought you'd be up. I know you'll have forgotten, so I've just rung to remind you that we have a visitor arriving today.'

Laszlo shook his head. Typical Jakob—ringing to check up on him. Jakob Frankel was the de Zsadany family lawyer, and a good man, but Laszlo couldn't imagine letting his guard down with him or any other outsider. Not any more: not after what had happened the last time.

'I know you won't believe me, Jakob, but I did actually remember it was happening today.'

He heard the lawyer laugh nervously.

'Excellent! I've arranged a car, but if you could be on hand to greet—?'

'Of course I will,' Laszlo interrupted testily, irritated by the tentative note in the lawyer's voice. He paused, aware that he sounded churlish. 'I want to be there,' he muttered roughly. 'And let me know if I can do anything else.' It was the nearest he got to an apology.

'Of course. Of course! But I'm sure that won't be necessary.' Jakob spoke hurriedly, his desire to end the conversation clearly overriding his normal deference.

Laszlo murmured non-committally. For most of his life Janos's hobby had seemed a strangely soulless and senseless exercise. But Annuska's death had changed that opinion as it had changed everything else.

After her funeral life at the castle had grown increasingly bleak. Janos had been in a state of shock, inconsolable with grief. But once the shock had worn off his misery had turned into a kind of depression—a lethargy which no amount of time seemed able to heal. Laszlo had been in despair; weeks and months had turned into years. Until slowly, and then with increasing momentum, his grandfather had become almost his old self.

The reason for his recovery, like all catalysts for change, had been wholly unexpected. A stack of letters between Annuska and Janos had reminded him of their mutual passion for art.

Tentatively, not daring to hope, Laszlo had encouraged his grandfather to revive his former hobby. To his surprise, Janos had begun to lose his listless manner and then, out of the blue, his grandfather had decided to have his sprawling collection catalogued. Seymour's auction house in London had been contacted and its flamboyant owner, Edmund Seymour, had duly been invited to visit Kastely Almasy.

Laszlo grimaced. His grandfather's happiness had overridden his own feeling but how on earth was he going to put up with this stranger in his home?

Jakob's voice broke into his thoughts.

'I mean, I know how you hate having people around—' There was a sudden awkward silence and then the lawyer cleared his throat. 'What I meant to say was—'

Laszlo interrupted him curtly. 'There are more

than thirty rooms at the castle, Jakob, so I think I'll be able to cope with one solitary guest, don't you?'

He felt a sudden, fierce stab of self-loathing. Seymour could stay for a year if it made his grandfather happy. And, really, what was a few weeks? Since Annuska's death time had ceased to matter. Nothing much mattered except healing his grandfather.

'I can manage,' he repeated gruffly.

'Of course...of course.' The lawyer laughed nervously. 'You might even enjoy it. In fact, Janos was only saying to me yesterday that this visit might be a good opportunity to invite some of the neighbours for drinks or dinner. The Szecsenyis are always good fun and they have a daughter around your age.'

In the early-morning light the room seemed suddenly grey and cold, like a tomb. Laszlo felt his fingers tighten around the handset as his heart started to pound out a drumroll of warning.

He took a shallow breath, groping for calm. 'I'll think about it,' he said finally. His tone was pleasant, but there was no mistaking the note of high-tensile steel in his voice. 'I mean, our guest may simply prefer paintings to people.'

He knew what his grandfather really wanted,

and why he had inveigled Jakob into suggesting it. Janos secretly longed to see his only grandchild married—to see Laszlo sharing his life with a soulmate. And why wouldn't he? After all, Janos himself had been blissfully happy during his forty-year marriage.

Laszlo's fingers curled into his palms. If only he could do it. If only he could marry a perfectly sweet, pretty girl like Agnes Szecsenyi. That would be worth more than fifty art collections to Janos.

But that was never going to happen. For he had a secret, and no matter how many dinner dates his grandfather engineered, a wife was most certainly not going to result from any of them.

'Now, you *have* read my notes properly, haven't you, Prue? Only you do have a tendency to skim...'

Pushing a strand of pale blonde hair out of her cloud-grey eyes, Prudence Elliot took a deep breath and counted slowly up to ten. Her plane had landed in Hungary only an hour ago, but this was the third time Uncle Edmund had rung her to see how she was doing: in other words, he was checking up on her.

Edmund paused. 'I don't want to sound like a

nag, but it's just… Well, I just wish I could be there with you…you *do* understand?'

His voice cut through her juddering, panicky thoughts and her anxiety was instantly replaced by guilt. Of course she understood. Her uncle had built up the auction house that bore his name from scratch. And today would have undoubtedly been the most important day of his career—the pinnacle of his life's work: cataloguing reclusive Hungarian billionaire Janos Almasy de Zsadany's legendary art collection.

With a lurch of fear, Prudence remembered the look of excitement and terror on Edmund's face when he'd been invited to the de Zsadany castle in Hungary. His words kept replaying in her head.

'The man's a modern Medici, Prue. Of course no one actually knows the exact contents of his collection. But a conservative valuation would be over a billion dollars.'

It should be Edmund with his thirty years of experience sitting in the back of the sleek, shark-nosed de Zsadany limousine. Not Prudence, who felt she could offer little more than her uncle's reputation by proxy. Only Edmund was in England, confined to bed, recovering from a major asthma attack.

Biting her lip, she glanced out of the window at the dark fields. She hadn't wanted to come. But she'd had no choice. Edmund owed money, and with debts mounting and interest accruing on those debts the business was in jeopardy. The fee from the de Zsadany job would balance the books, but the de Zsadany family lawyer had been adamant that work must start immediately. And so, reluctantly, she'd agreed to go to Hungary.

She heard Edmund sigh down the phone.

'I'm sorry, Prue,' he said slowly. 'You shouldn't have to put up with my nagging when you've been so good about all this.'

Instantly she felt ashamed. Edmund was like a father to her. He had given her everything: a home, a family, security and even a job. She wasn't about to let him down now, in his hour of need.

Taking a deep breath, she tried to inject some confidence into her voice. 'Please try not to worry, Edmund. If I need anything at all I'll ring you. But I'll be fine. I promise.'

He rang off and gratefully Prudence leant back against the leather upholstery and closed her eyes until, in what felt like no time at all, the car began to slow. She opened her eyes. Two tall wrought-iron gates swung smoothly open to let the limousine pass, and within minutes she was looking up at a huge, grey stone castle straight out of a picture book.

Later she would realise that she had no memory of how she got from the car to the castle. She remembered only that somehow she had found herself in a surprisingly homely sitting room, lit softly by a collection of table lamps and the glow of a log fire. She was about to sit down on a faded Knole Sofa when she noticed the painting.

Her heart started to pound. Stepping closer, she reached out with one trembling hand and touched the frame lightly, and then her eyes made a slow tour of the walls. She felt light-headed—as though she had woken up in dream. There were two Picassos—pink period—a delightfully exuberant Kandinsky, a Rembrandt portrait that would have sent Edmund into a state of near ecstasy, and a pair of exquisite Lucian Freud etchings of a sleeping whippet.

She was still in a state of moderate shock when an amused-sounding voice behind her said softly, 'Please—take a closer look. I'm afraid the poor things get completely ignored by the rest of us.'

Prudence turned scarlet. To be caught snooping around someone's sitting room like some sort of burglar was bad enough, but when that someone was your host, and one of the richest men in Europe, it was mortifying.

'I'm so—so sorry,' she stammered, turning round. 'What must you…?' The remainder of her apology died in her throat, the words colliding into one another with a series of shuddering jolts as her world imploded. For it was not Janos Almasy de Zsadany standing there but Laszlo Cziffra.

Laszlo Cziffra. Once his name had tasted hot and sweet in her mouth; now it was bitter on her tongue. She felt her insides twist in pain as around her the room seemed to collapse and fold in on itself like a house of cards. It couldn't be Laszlo—it just couldn't. But it was, and she stared at him mutely, reeling from the shock of his perfection.

With his high cheekbones, sleek black hair and burning amber eyes, he was almost the same boy she had fallen in love with seven years ago: her beautiful Romany boy. Only he most certainly wasn't hers any more; nor was he a boy. Now he was unmistakably a man: tall, broad-shouldered, intensely male, and with a suggestion of conformity that his younger self had lacked. Prudence shivered. But it was his eyes that had changed the most. Once, on seeing her, they would have burnt with the fierce lambent fire of passion. Now they were as cold and lifeless as ash.

She felt breathless, almost faint, and her hand moved involuntarily to her throat. Laszlo had been her first love—her first lover. He had been like sunlight and storms. She had never wanted anything or anyone more than him. And he had noticed *her*. Chosen *her* with a certainty that had left her breathless, replete, exultant. She had felt immortal. The knowledge of his love had swelled inside her—an immutable truth as permanent as the sun rising and setting.

Or so she'd believed seven years ago.

Only she'd been wrong. His focus on her—for that was what it had been—had burnt white-hot, fire-bright, and then faded fast like a supernova.

Prudence swallowed. It had been the ugliest thing that had happened to her. After the fierce bliss of what she'd believed was his love, that disorientating darkness had felt like death itself. And now, like a ghost from paradise lost, here he was, defying all logic and reason.

Surely he couldn't be real? And if he was real then what was he doing *here*? It didn't make any sense. She stared at him, groping for some kind of answer. Her stomach lurched as she remembered the last time she'd seen him: being pushed into the back of a police car, his face dark and defiant.

Laszlo didn't belong in a place like this. And yet here he was. Standing there, as though he owned the place.

She felt her stomach lurch. In the back of her mind, pushed down in the darkness, she'd always imagined that he'd drifted into bad ways. So to watch him saunter into the room was almost more than her brain could fathom. Helplessly, she racked her brain for some shred of explanation.

'Wh—what are you doing here?' she stammered, her voice sounding small and shrunken, like a soul facing purgatory.

Laszlo stared at Prudence, his handsome face cold and blank. But inside it was as though he was falling from a great height. His mind was racing, explanations tumbling over one another, each one more desperate and untenable than the last. And all the time, like a silent movie, the short, doomed pretence of their love played out before his eyes.

Aware that he was playing for time, he felt a rush of anger. But words had literally failed him—for he had blotted out all traces of her so completely that just looking at her made him feel dizzy.

'I could ask you the same question,' he murmured.

And then, with shock, he remembered that it had been only that morning that his hunger-fuelled brain had conjured up her memory. He shivered as the hairs stood up on the back of his neck and he remembered the cry of the owl he had heard earlier. Had he somehow summoned her here?

The part of his mind not numb with shock pushed the suggestion away irritably: of course he hadn't. Clearly she hadn't come looking for him, for her own shock was unmistakable. So what exactly was she doing here?

Eyes narrowing, he stared assessingly at her and waited for answers.

White-faced, Prudence stared back at him dazedly. She must have fallen down a rabbit hole, for what other explanation could there be? Why else was Laszlo Cziffra here in this isolated castle in the Hungarian countryside? Unless—her blood turned cold—could he be working for Mr de Zsadany?

Her mind cringed from the possibility and, remembering his blank-eyed indifference when she'd told him she was leaving him, she felt suddenly sick. But that had been seven years ago. Surely after all this time they could treat each other with at the very least a polite neutrality? But instead of cool curiosity, he was watching her with a sort of icy contempt.

'I don't understand—' She broke off, the colour draining from her cheeks as he walked slowly across the faded Persian carpet towards her. 'What are you doing here?' she said again. 'You *can't* be here.'

Watching the shock on her face turn to horror as he approached, Laszlo felt the floor yaw beneath him like a wave-tossed ship. But he had no intention of revealing to Prudence how strongly he was affected by her presence. Or her evident dismay at seeing him again.

Breathing deeply, he steadied himself. 'But I am,' he said slowly. 'Why are you trembling, *pireni*?'

She tried to ignore it. Just as she was trying to ignore how handsome he was and his nerve-jangling nearness. But the familiar word of endearment seemed to grow to a roar inside her head, drowning out her answer to his question.

For what felt like a lifetime they stood, staring at one another in silence, as they had done a hundred...a thousand times before.

The man's voice, when it came, startled both of them.

'Ah, there you are! I'm sorry I'm late. The traffic was terrible.'

A plumpish, middle-aged man, with thick, dull blonde hair and a panicked expression on his face, hurried into the room. Turning to Prudence, he shuffled some files under his arm and held out his hand.

'I'm so sorry to have missed you at the airport, Miss Elliot. You got my message, though?'

Still speechless with shock, Prudence nodded. She had felt a momentary spasm of relief at the man's arrival. But now it would appear that her relief was premature. For his words had made it painfully clear to her that Laszlo's presence was a shock only to *her*.

The man glanced cautiously at Laszlo and cleared his throat. 'I see you two have already met. So let me introduce myself. Jakob Frankel. I work for the law firm that represents Mr de Zsadany. May I say on behalf of the family how grateful we all are for you stepping in at the last moment. It was really very kind of you.'

Laszlo felt his guts twist. His brain was struggling to give meaning to what was happening. Jakob *had* told him that Edmund Seymour was ill and that someone else was coming in his place. Typically, he'd forgotten—for one stranger was no better or worse than another. But suddenly

Jakob's words seemed to take on a new and wholly unpalatable significance: Seymour's replacement was *Prudence Elliot*. And that meant she would be living under his roof for the foreseeable future!

'It's my pleasure,' Prudence said hoarsely.

The lawyer nodded and, looking nervously from Prudence to Laszlo, said, 'Everyone is most grateful.'

Prudence smiled weakly and opened her mouth to speak but Laszlo interrupted her.

'Miss Elliot could buy her own castle with the fee we're paying her. I don't think she needs our gratitude as well.'

Flinching at the undertone of hostility in his voice, Prudence felt rather than saw Laszlo's dark, probing gaze turn towards her. Her breath, suddenly sharp and serrated, tore at her throat and she touched her neck nervously. She still had no idea what he was doing here but he must be important, for the lawyer was clearly deferring to him. The thought somehow exhausted her, and she felt suddenly on the verge of tears.

This wasn't supposed to be happening. It was bad enough feeling out of her depth professionally. But now there was Laszlo, staring at her with those cold, dismissive eyes, and all she could think was that he could still make her feel like nothing. How he had made her feel like nothing seven years ago. Swallowing, she gritted her teeth. At least she'd fought for their relationship; he, on the other hand, had been too busy doing whatever he'd done to get himself arrested.

And she *wasn't* nothing. In his words, she was being paid enough to buy a castle to do this job and that was what she was there to do. Her job. It didn't matter that once upon a time, her love hadn't been good enough for him.

Lifting her chin, she turned towards the lawyer. 'You're very kind, Mr Frankel,' she said clearly. 'Thank you for allowing me to come. This is a marvellous opportunity for me. I just hope I can live up to your expectations.'

'Oh, I wouldn't worry about that,' Laszlo murmured softly. 'We have very low expectations.'

There was another long, tense moment of silence and then Frankel gave a nervous laugh. 'What Mr Cziffra is trying to say—'

'Is that Miss Elliot and I can take it from here,' Laszlo finished smoothly.

The lawyer looked at him doubtfully. 'You can?'

'I think I can manage.' Laszlo's voice was as cold

and flat as an Arctic ice floe and Prudence shivered as Frankel nodded, his plump face flushed.

'Of course,' he said hastily. 'Of course.' He turned towards Prudence.

'You'll be in safe hands, Miss Elliot! After Mr de Zsadany, no one knows more about the collection than his grandson.'

The shock was like a jolt of electricity.

Prudence felt her whole body still and then start to shake. The room was spinning at the edge of her vision. Janos Almasy de Zsadany was Laszlo's grandfather! But how could he be? Janos Almasy de Zsadany was a billionaire several times over. Laszlo was a Romany—a traveller who lived in a trailer. How could they possibly be related?

With an almost painful stab of hope she wondered if she had misheard Frankel and she turned to Laszlo, expecting, praying he would still be staring at her with the same cold, uninterested expression. But she saw instead that he was staring at her with a look of pitying scorn and horror.

Her stomach convulsed with fear. Frankel was telling the truth.

Heart thumping, feeling dizzy and sick, she glanced numbly at the lawyer. But he seemed unaware of the turmoil he had created with his simple statement of fact. Fighting her misery, she glanced back at Laszlo. There was no denial on his face—no embarrassment or confusion, and she stared at him, unable to ignore, even in her misery, his luminous, impossible beauty.

He looked up and she flinched as he met her gaze, the softness of his mouth only seeming to emphasise the hard challenge in his eyes.

Frankel coughed. 'Right. In that case I'll be on my way. Goodnight, Miss Elliot! I'll see myself out, Mr Cziffra.'

'Thank you, Frankel.' Laszlo stared steadily at Prudence, his eyes glittering like shards of yellow glass. 'Enjoy the rest of your evening. And don't worry. I'll take good care of Miss Elliot.'

Prudence felt her stomach turn to liquid as Laszlo turned towards her and nodded.

'I promise I'll give her my full and undivided attention.'

The table lamps felt suddenly like spotlights, and although the room was warm she felt cold and shivery. She watched Frankel leave with a mounting sense of dread, every nerve in her body straining to breaking point. She wanted to run after the lawyer and beg him to stay but her body was rooted to the spot. Numbly, she stared at the paintings on the wall. Just moments ago they had given her such innocent pleasure. But not any more. Now they seemed like cruel-eyed onlookers, mocking her stupidity.

The anaesthetic of shock and bewilderment was starting to wear off and she felt a sudden stabbing surge of irritation. Okay, it was awkward and stressful for both of them to be thrown together like this, but surely she had a far greater reason to be upset than him? Surely she deserved some answers here? Her lip curled. In fact, how could he just stand there and not offer one word of explanation?

Glancing at his expressionless face, she gritted her teeth. Quite easily, it would appear. Her chest tightened. He hadn't changed a bit. He was still putting the onus on her to resolve everything. As though he were a witness rather than a central protagonist in what was happening.

'Pretending I'm not here isn't going to make this go away!' she said slowly. Willing herself to stay as cool as she sounded, she lifted her chin and met his gaze. 'We need to sort this out.'

Laszlo stared at her. '"Sort this out"?' he echoed softly. His mouth tightened as he suppressed a humourless laugh. There was nothing *to* sort out!

Except out of which door he would throw her! 'Is that what we need to do?' His eyes met hers. 'So. You're Seymour's replacement?' he said coolly.

Heart thumping against her ribcage, Prudence nodded. Keeping her eyes straight ahead, she cleared her throat. 'And you're Mr de Zsadany's grandson!'

She fell silent and waited for his answer. But he did nothing more than nod. Turning her head, she clenched her fists: the words *incorrigible* and *impossible* were ricocheting inside her brain. Was that it, then? No explanations. Not one word to acknowledge the impact and implication of those words.

As though reading her mind, Laszlo sighed. His eyes looked through her and past her as he spoke. 'My mother was Zsofia Almasy de Zsadany. She was Janos's daughter and only child.'

It was like hearing a marble statue speak and her heart flinched at the chill in his voice.

'She met my father, Istvan, when she was sixteen. He was seventeen, a Kalderash Roma. Both their families opposed the match but they loved each other so much that nothing could keep them apart.'

His eyes gleamed and she felt a jolt of pain at the accusatory barb of his words.

'They were married and I was born nine months later.'

Prudence stared at him numbly. Who *was* this Laszlo? And what had he been doing living in a shabby trailer in England? Had he been rebelling? Or estranged from the de Zsadanys? Her head was swimming with questions. From knowing next to nothing about him she suddenly had so much information she could hardly take it all in. But her heart contracted as she realised that even the small things he had shared with her had been half-truths.

'Why were you there? In England, I mean?'

He frowned. 'After my parents died I spent time with both my families. My grandfather wanted me to go to school. To be educated. So I stayed in Hungary during term-time, and in the holidays I went and visited my father's family, wherever they happened to be living.' His eyes gleamed remorselessly. 'I wanted to be loyal to both my mother *and* my father.'

She forced herself to meet his gaze. 'I see,' she said slowly. 'But you didn't want to be open and honest with me?' She felt a sudden rise in tension as his eyes slid slowly and assessingly over her rigid frame.

'No. I did not,' he said finally.

Prudence gaped at him, her pledge to stay calm and detached now completely forgotten. 'Didn't you think it might have been better, not to say *fairer*, to share the whole truth with me?' she said furiously. 'You know—the fact that your grand-father was one of the richest men in Europe? And that you lived in a castle surrounded by priceless works of art?'

He looked away from her and shrugged. Prudence felt almost giddy with rage. How dare he just stand there and shrug at her? As if it didn't matter that he'd lied to her. As if *she* didn't matter.

'What difference would it have made?' he said flatly. 'There were lots of facts you didn't know about me—why focus on that one?' His face twisted. 'Unless, of course, it wasn't the truth you wanted to share. Maybe there were other things you'd have liked to share. Like my grandfather's money.'

The breath seemed to snarl up in her throat. 'How can you say that?' She stepped towards him, her body shaking with anger. 'How can you even suggest—?' Her head was spinning, nerves humming with rage and frustration. 'Don't you dare try and twist this, Laszlo. You lied to me!'

Laszlo's face was suddenly as pale and rigid as bone and she had to curl her fingers into her hands to stop herself from flinching at the hostility in his eyes.

'I didn't lie,' he said coldly. 'I *am* half-Romany and I *did* live in a trailer.'

'Oh, that's okay, then,' Prudence said sarcastically. 'Maybe it was your other half. The half that lived in a castle. Perhaps *he* lied to me?'

Anger was bubbling up inside her, her breath burning her throat. *She* wasn't the one who'd lied about who she was. She winced as her nails dug into her skin. Had he actually told her the truth about anything?

Laszlo met her gaze. 'You believed what you wanted to believe.'

Prudence shook her head in disbelief. 'I believed what you encouraged me to believe,' she said furiously. 'There's a difference.'

There was a dangerous silence and then his eyes narrowed.

'You're missing the point, Prudence. It doesn't matter what someone believes if they don't have faith.' His voice was ragged, frayed with a bitterness she had never heard before. 'Without that it's all just words.'

She sucked in a breath. 'Yes, it is. *Your* words. The lies you told me.' Her heart was pounding; her hands were tight fists against her sides. 'Don't try and turn this into some philosophical debate, Laszlo. I'm upset because you lied to me and you took away my choices.'

'So now we're even,' he said coldly.

CHAPTER TWO

SHE STARED AT him blankly. Even? *Even!*

'What that's supposed to mean?' She flung the words at him, wishing they were sticks or stones or better still bricks. But he didn't reply. Instead he made an impatient sound and she watched helplessly as his face closed tight like a trap. Her muscles were aching with the effort of not picking up a lamp and beating him to death with it. How could he *do* that? Just switch off in the middle of a conversation and take himself outside of it?

Feeling a familiar cold, paralysing panic, she wrapped her arms around herself. But of course she didn't need him to answer anyway. She knew exactly what he was talking about.

An undertow of defiance tugged at her frustration and slowly she shook her head. 'No, Laszlo. If you're talking about the fact that I ended our relationship, then we are *not* even. Not even close to being even.'

Her whole body was suddenly shaking and she

wrapped her arms more tightly around herself. Walking away from Laszlo and from her romantic hopes and dreams had been hard—one of the hardest things she'd ever done—and it had taken every ounce of willpower she'd had. But if he'd wanted to, if he'd wanted her, he could have stopped her; she'd given him every chance to change her mind. Only he'd barely uttered a word when she'd told him that she was leaving him. Certainly not the sort she'd craved. He'd let her go and that had been his choice.

A sudden, suffocating misery reared up inside her as, with a shudder, she remembered just how cold and unapproachable he'd been.

She stood rooted to the spot, numbed and struck dumb at her own stupidity. No wonder he'd been so secretive—smuggling her into his trailer and carefully sidestepping her requests to meet his family. Fool that she was, she'd been too dizzy with love, too in thrall to the way her body had softened and transformed beneath his touch, to wonder why. Besides, she'd been flattered at the start, at least, for she'd believed that he wanted her all to himself. He'd stolen her heart and her virginity in quick succession and all the while he'd been living a lie.

She looked at him wearily. But why did this lie

matter, really? After all, she couldn't change the past. Or change the fact that he hadn't loved her enough to fight for her. Her mouth twisted. This discussion was a dead end. There was no point in trying to talk about their relationship now: it was seven years too late. And besides, she had a new life now. Maybe not the one she'd been hoping for, but a good life, and she wasn't about to let him pick up her world and smash it to smithereens.

Her pulse fluttered into life and she glanced at the door, wishing she could go back in time to the moment before she'd walked through it. And then, with a start, she remembered that even if that had been possible it simply wasn't an option. Edmund needed this job. That was why she had come to Hungary. And she needed to focus on that fact and not get sidetracked into a post-mortem of her romantic past.

She took a calming breath. The cataloguing was more important than her feelings. Not that she had any feelings for Laszlo any more. At least not any that should get in the way of what was essentially a job like any other. Their relationship was history and, while clearly she would never have chosen to meet him again, let alone work with him, there was no reason not to treat him like any other client—albeit one who was difficult, bordering on the socially inept.

Fighting down the urge to bolt through the door, she lifted her chin and met his gaze. She wasn't going to let his inability to let go of the past upset her. She would be calm and efficient—a detached professional.

'This is getting us nowhere, Laszlo,' she said firmly. 'I'm here to do a job for you and your grandfather.'

Biting her lip, she paused, her muscles tightening again. Did Janos know about her relationship with his grandson? That could be awkward. But then her body relaxed. Somehow she didn't think so. It was a long time ago, and they'd never met, and Laszlo had probably had hundreds of girlfriends since her. Her cheeks grew suddenly hot and quickly she pushed that thought away.

'I know he wants to start on the cataloguing as soon as possible, so why don't we put aside our differences and try and concentrate on making that happen for him? Can we do that? Can we call a truce?' She gave a small, tight smile and clenched her hands into fists to stop herself from crossing her fingers.

Laszlo stared at her speculatively. She wanted

this job. It was obvious from the conciliatory note in her voice and the slight increase in tension around her shoulders. His gaze drifted hungrily over her neck to the pulse beating in the hollow at the base of her throat. To anyone who didn't know her she looked like the perfect English Rose, pale and demure. But he knew the other Prudence. The one beneath that calm, poised exterior, who had wrapped herself around him with passion and fervour. That contrast, and the knowledge that he alone possessed that other, hidden Prudence, had excited him unbearably. With a spasm of disbelief, he realised it still did.

Feeling his body stiffen, he lifted his gaze and smiled at her almost mockingly. 'Since you put it so nicely—'

She stared at him warily. She hadn't expected him to come round so easily. But then, with Laszlo you never knew what to expect. 'Thank you,' she said stiffly. 'I must say I'm a bit surprised—'

He smiled coolly. 'I know how much women love surprises.'

Nodding, she forced herself to breathe slowly. Perhaps she could make this work. She just needed to stay focused on what was important: the fact that Laszlo was nothing more than a client. She looked up and found him watching her. A tingle of heat ran down her spine. She could almost see his desire—feel him wrapping it round her like a dark velvet cloak.

Her cheeks were burning. Quickly, before the sudden softness in his eyes could rattle her even more, she looked away. She was here to work and it didn't matter that she and Laszlo had once shared a passion so pagan, so consuming, that the outside world had ceased to exist. Now their relationship needed to work only on a business level.

She met his eyes. 'And I know men hate delays.' She paused and cleared her throat. 'So I suggest we discuss what happens now.'

Laszlo stared at her. A peony-pink flush had crept over the skin on her throat and his gaze drifted down over the pale grey blouse that clung to the soft swell of her breasts, then lower still to where the smooth downward curve of her hips and waist pressed tight against the fabric of her skirt. She was so close they were practically touching and, breathing in the familiar scent of jasmine, he found himself almost paralysed with longing again.

Breathing in sharply, he gritted his teeth. He had spent so long hating her, hating what she had done to him, that he had never supposed that he might still want her.

And yet apparently he did.

He stared at her, confused. He wanted her. But he also wanted to punish her. And yet even that wasn't wholly true, for he couldn't help but admire her. After all, how many other women—particularly one as shy and unworldly as Prudence—would stand their ground in this situation? Not that it surprised him. She had always possessed that quality of being in a state of quiescence, of teetering on the edge. His jaw tensed as her misty grey gaze rested on his face. Only now was not the time to be thinking about Prudence's finer qualities. Better to concentrate on her flaws.

'You tell me. Talking was always your thing, wasn't it? For me, actions speak louder than words.'

He watched colour creep across her cheeks. Saw the moment that she relaxed, the tension leaving her body, making it softer and more vulnerable.

Prudence felt her cheeks grow warm. She needed no reminder of how eloquent his actions had been. Particularly not now, when she needed to keep her thoughts in some semblance of order. But his smile was like a beam of sunlight breaking through cloud. She just wanted to follow it...place herself in its path.

Focus, she told herself firmly. She cleared her throat and began to talk quickly. 'As I said before, I know how keen your grandfather is to begin the cataloguing. So I think we should push on with the original timeframe.'

He stepped towards her and she tensed, her body suddenly a helix of tendon and muscle.

'You're the expert,' he murmured.

Blushing, Prudence swallowed. His voice was such a captivating mix of soft and seductive. She felt heat begin to build inside her and for one brief moment allowed herself to remember the touch of his fingers, travelling over her skin with the virtuosity of a concert pianist. How the rippling rhythms of their bodies had quickened and inter-twined to a breathless cadence.

Prudence took a deep breath. Surely she couldn't still actually find him attractive? She must have more sense than that. But what had sense got to do with lust? No woman alive could stand next to Laszlo Cziffra and feel nothing.

Somewhere in the castle a door slammed and Prudence started forward with surprise. For a moment her hands grazed his chest as she swayed against him and then, breathing unsteadily, she teetered backwards. They were standing inches apart now. He was so close she could feel the heat of his skin. Her heart was pounding as though she'd been running and her body was trembling helplessly. He smelt of newly mown hay and rain-soaked earth and she felt almost dazed with longing as every inch of her reacted to him.

'Castles were built to keep out arrows and cannon fire. Not draughts,' he said drily.

Still horrified by the revelation that her body apparently had no loyalty to her heart, Prudence dragged her gaze away, hoping that he hadn't noticed or, worse, correctly interpreted her physical response to him.

'Weren't they?' she mumbled, her cheeks flushing. 'Wh—what was I saying? Oh, yes. The time-frame. Three weeks is a typical estimate for a preliminary assessment. It's important to be thorough at that stage.' She frowned. 'And don't worry. If I have any problems I can speak to Mr Seymour. In fact, I'll be in close contact with him the entire time.' She gave a small, tight smile. 'I find it helpful to have another point of view. For clarity.'

Her smile faded and she stared at him nervously, aware of a sudden stillness in him, a slight narrowing of his eyes, although she couldn't quite understand what had changed. But then, why should she care? She was here to work, and Laszlo's moods were no longer her concern.

Clearing her throat, she straightened her shoulders and forced herself to ignore the undertow of apprehension tugging at the back of her mind. 'A-and obviously I'm happy to discuss any concerns Mr de Zsadany has,' she stammered. His eyes clashed with hers and despite herself she felt another twinge of foreboding.

'Obviously...' he said coolly. 'I know how you love to discuss problems.'

Her heart was thumping hard. There it was again: a tiny but deliberate dig. He was taking what was nothing more than a casual, unpremeditated remark and making it something personal, to do with the past. *Their* past. She felt sudden swift anger. Hadn't they agreed to call a truce? This was going to be hard enough as it was, without him making a difficult situation worse with his snippy double-edged comments.

Her mind was so churned up with emotion it took her another couple of moments before she understood just *how* difficult the situation was going to be. For it wasn't as if she was just going to *work* with Laszlo—her blood seemed to still in her veins—she was going to have to live with him too.

A tremor grew at the back of her neck. Of course she would have to live with him. But not like this. Not dreading his every remark—not deliberately having to misunderstand his every insinuation. She needed to make it clear now that she would not tolerate being treated like that.

'I don't *like* discussing problems.' Returning his gaze coldly, she lifted her chin. 'It's just that I think communication is key to a successful relationship.'

She had meant to sound assured, without being overtly confrontational. But she knew the moment she spoke that it was the wrong thing to say. For he went entirely still and his eyes locked onto hers like an infrared missile seeking its target.

Swaying, she took a faltering step backwards. 'I didn't mean us—'

'Don't bother! I already know pretty much all there is to know about your views on relationships.'

Watching the shock and confusion bloom on her face, Laszlo felt a surge of satisfaction.

His voice was little more than a rasp. 'You explained them to me in great detail when you walked out on me—*Prudence.*'

She flinched as he turned towards her and spat her name into the air as though it were a poison he had inadvertently swallowed.

'In fact...' He paused, his lip curling with contempt. 'You made it abundantly clear how pitiable I was to have ever imagined that our relationship might work, given the range and depth of my flaws.'

'N-no. I didn't—' Prudence began shakily, shocked and unnerved by the level of venom in his voice. But her voice died as he stepped towards her and she saw real anger in his eyes.

'Oh, but you did.' His face was tight with emotion. 'Only you were wrong. They weren't *my* flaws. They were yours!' he ground out between gritted teeth. 'You were just too weak and snobbish—'

'I was *not* weak and snobbish.' The injustice of his words melted her shock and suddenly she was coldly furious. 'I just didn't want to pretend any more.'

'Pretend what? That you loved me?' His face was blunt, angular with hostility.

Liquid misery trickled through her. 'That we had anything in common.'

He shook his head. 'Like loyalty, you mean?

Maybe you're right. We certainly felt differently about *that*!'

'You don't need to tell me about the differences between us,' she snapped, stung into speech by the censure in his voice. 'I know all about them. They're why our relationship didn't work. Why it could never have worked.'

Her throat tightened as he looked at her coldly.

'Our relationship didn't fail because we were different. It failed because you cared more about those differences than you did about me,' he snarled. 'Tell me, *pireni*, how are you finding my communication skills now? Am I making myself clear enough?'

Her heart gave a sudden jerk as abruptly he turned and walked towards the fireplace.

For a moment she stood frozen, gazing speechlessly at his back. Anger was building inside her, displacing all other feeling, and suddenly she crossed the room and yanked him round to face her.

'That's not true! I *did* care—' She broke off. Rage, hot and unstoppable, choked her words. 'Don't you dare try and tell me what I felt.' She set her jaw, her eyes narrowing. 'If I cared about the differences between us it was because, yes, I thought they mattered. Unlike you, I like to talk about the things that matter to me. And, crazy though this may sound, I try and tell the truth. But what would *you* know about that? The truth is like a foreign language to you.'

She watched his eyes darken with fury, the pupils seeming almost to engulf the golden irises.

'The truth?' he said savagely. 'You left me because you thought I wasn't good enough for you. *That's* the truth. You're just too much of a coward to admit it.'

Silently, Prudence shook her head. Not only because she was disagreeing with him but because she was too angry to speak. She hadn't even known she could feel that angry.

Finally, she found her voice. 'How dare you talk to me about the truth when we're standing here in this castle? *Your* castle. A castle I didn't even know existed until today.' Her eyes flashed with anger. 'And just because I wanted to talk about the leaks in the trailer and the fact that we didn't have enough money to buy food for more than a couple of days didn't mean I thought you weren't good enough!'

'Those things shouldn't have mattered. They didn't matter to *me*,' Laszlo snarled.

'I know!' she snarled back at him. 'But they did to me. And you can't punish me for that fact. Or for the fact that it worried me: how we felt differently about things. We disagreed about stuff and that was going to be a problem for us sooner or later, only you wouldn't admit it,' she raged at him. 'So it wasn't me who was a coward. It was you.'

She took a sudden step backwards as he moved towards her; his face was in shadow but the fury beneath his skin was luminous.

'I am not the coward here, Prudence,' he said quietly, and his dispassionate tone was frighteningly at odds with the menacing gleam in his eyes.

Prudence felt her insides lurch. Beneath the chill of his gaze her courage and powers of speech wilted momentarily and she felt suddenly defeated. Suddenly she didn't want to talk any more. What was the point? Judging by the last twenty minutes it would only hurt more than it healed.

When at last she spoke, her voice was defeated. 'This is going nowhere,' she said wearily. 'I know you're angry. We both are. But can't we just put our past behind us? At least until after the cataloguing is complete?'

Laszlo stared at her, his eyes glittering with fury. 'The *cataloguing*? Do you know what my grandfather's collection means to him? Or why he decided to have it catalogued?' He shook his head. 'After everything that's happened between us, do you really think I'd trust *you*, of all people—?' He broke off and breathed out unsteadily.

Prudence felt a stab of fear. What was he trying to say? 'But you can,' she said shakily. 'I'll do a good job. You have my word.'

He winced as though she had ripped a plaster from a scab. 'Your *word*?' he repeated. He tilted his head. 'Your word...' he said again.

And this time the contempt on his face felt like a hammer blow. Her mouth had gone dry.

'I—I only meant—' she stammered, but he cut across her words with a voice like a flick knife.

'It doesn't matter what you meant. We both know that your word is worthless.'

'What are you talking about?'

Balling his fists, feeling sick to his stomach, Laszlo shook his head. He felt an odd rushing sensation in his head, like a sort of vertigo, and words and memories hurtled past him like debris from an explosion. What kind of woman *was* she? He had long known her to be snobbish and weak-minded, but this—this refusal to acknowledge what she'd done—

His jaw tightened.

'I honoured you with a gift. The most important gift a man can give to a woman. I made you my wife and you threw it in my face.'

Prudence gaped at him, shock washing over in waves. She opened her mouth to deny his claim but the words clogged her throat. His *wife*? Surely he didn't really think that they were actually *married*? Her heart was pounding; the palms of her hands felt suddenly damp. Married? That was ridiculous! Insane!

Dazedly she thought back to that day when she'd been led, giggling and blindfolded, to his great-uncle's trailer. Laszlo had been waiting for her. She felt a shiver run down her spine at the memory, for he'd looked heartbreakingly handsome and so serious she had wanted to cry. They'd sworn their love and commitment to one another, and his great-uncle had spoken some words in Romany, and then they had eaten some bread and some salt.

Coming out of her reverie, she stared hard at him wordlessly. There had been no actual marriage. It had been no more real than his love for her. But it had been part of the fantasy of their love. And now he was destroying that fantasy. Taking the memory of something beautiful, innocent and spontaneous and turning it into a means of hurting her.

Her vision blurred and she felt suddenly giddy, as though she were teetering on the edge of a cliff-face. 'You're despicable! Why are you doing this? Why are you trying to ruin that day?'

'Ruin it?' His features contorted with fury. 'You're the one who did that. By walking out on our marriage.'

Her pulse was fluttering and despite her best efforts her voice sounded high and jerky. 'We're not married,' she said tightly. 'Marriages are more than just words and kisses. This is just another of your lies—'

Her voice trailed off at the expression of derision on his face.

'No. This is just the ultimate proof of how little you understood or respected my way of life. For you, my being Romany was just some whimsical lifestyle choice.' He watched the blood suffuse her face and felt a spasm of pain. 'You liked it that I was different—an outsider. But you didn't expect or want me to stay like that. You thought I'd just throw it off, like a fancy dress costume, and become "normal" when it came to the rest of our lives.' His eyes hardened. 'That's when you started whining about the mess and the moving around. But that's what we do. It's what *I* do.'

'Except when you're living in a castle,' she said shakily.

His gaze held hers. 'You're going off topic, *pireni*. It doesn't matter where I lived then or where I live now. We're still married. I'm still your husband. And you're my wife.'

She felt a stab of shock—both at the vehemence in his voice and at the sudden spread of treacherous heat at his possessive words.

Turning her head, she swallowed. 'What happened in that trailer wasn't a wedding, Laszlo. There were no guests. No vicar. No witnesses. We didn't give each other rings. We didn't even sign anything. It wasn't a wedding at all and I'm not your wife.'

Laszlo forced himself to stay calm. He had too much pride to let her see that her horrified denial had reopened a wound that had never fully healed—a wound that had left him hollowed out with misery and humiliation.

Shaking his head, he gave a humourless laugh. 'Oh, believe me, *pireni*, I wish you weren't— but you are.' His fingers curled into the palms of his hands. 'In my culture a wedding is a private

affair between a man and wife. We don't register
the marriage, and the only authority that's needed
for it to be recognised is the consent of the bride
and groom.'

Prudence felt a vertigo-like flash of fear. She
shook her head. 'We're not married,' she croaked.
'Not in the eyes of the law.'

The change in him was almost imperceptible.
She might even have missed the slight rigidity
about his jawline had the contempt in his eyes not
seared her skin.

'Not your law, maybe.' He felt a hot, overpow-
ering rage. 'But in mine. Yes, we were married—
and we still are.'

Closing her eyes, she felt a sudden, inexplicable
sense of panic. Laszlo clearly believed what he was
saying. Whilst she might have viewed the cere-
mony as a curious but charming dress rehearsal for
the vintage-style white wedding she'd been planning, the marriage had been real to him. Nausea
gripped her stomach. What did it really matter if
there was no certificate? It didn't mean that the
vows they'd made were any less valid or binding.

Heat scorched her skin. *What had she done?* She
looked up and his gaze held hers, and she saw that
he was furious, fighting for control.

'Laszlo, I didn't—'

His voice was barely audible but it scythed through her words and on through her skin and bone, slicing into her heart.

'This conversation is over. I'm sorry you had a wasted trip but your services are no longer required.'

Prudence looked at him in confusion, her face bleached of colour. 'I—I don't understand…' she stammered. 'What do you mean?'

Laszlo rounded on her coldly. 'What do I *mean*?' he echoed. 'I mean that you're fired—dismissed, sacked. Your contract is terminated and this meeting is over. As of this moment I never want to see your face again.' He turned back towards the fire. 'So why don't you take your bags, turn around and get out of my house? *Now.*'

CHAPTER THREE

PRUDENCE FELT THE floor tilt towards her. She reached out and steadied herself against the back of an armchair. 'You can't do that,' she said slowly. 'You can't just fire me.'

'Oh, but I can.'

Laszlo turned and looked at her, full in the face, and a shudder raced through her as she saw to her horror that he meant it.

'But that's so unfair!' Her voice seemed to echo around the room and she gazed at him helplessly.

'I don't care.'

He spoke flatly, his jaw tightening, and with a spasm of pain she knew that he didn't. Knew too that it wouldn't matter what she said or did and that it had probably never mattered. She had lost the job the moment Laszlo walked into the room. She just hadn't realised that fact until now.

She stared at him, shock and disbelief choking her words of objection. But inside her head there was a deafening cacophony of protest. He couldn't fire her. What would she tell Edmund? And what about their debts to the bank and the insurance company?

'No.'

The word burst from her lips like a flying spear. Laszlo stared at her calmly. Firing her seemed to have lanced his fury and he seemed more puzzled than angry at her outburst.

'No?' he murmured softly. 'No, what?'

She glared at him, her cheeks flooding with angry colour. 'No, I won't leave. I know I made a mistake, but it all happened years ago—and any-way you can't fire me for that. Apart from any-thing else it's got nothing to do with my ability to do this job.'

'It's got *everything* to do with your ability to do this job,' Laszlo said coldly. 'You lack convic-tion and loyalty and I don't employ people with-out those qualities.'

Prudence sucked in a breath, hating him more than she had ever hated him before. 'Stop it!' she hissed. He was so self-righteous and hypocriti-cal. How dare he act as if he had the moral high ground? He'd lied to her. And he was the one who'd broken the law and been arrested for who knew what! Perhaps he should examine his own failings first instead of focusing on hers.

She opened her mouth to tell him so and then closed it again. There was so much history in this room already. Why add more? She breathed out slowly.

'Stop sitting in judgement on me! You're not some innocent victim here, Laszlo. You lied. Maybe that doesn't matter to you, but it does to me.' She stopped, her breathing ragged. 'Only I'm not using it to get at you. I wouldn't stoop that low.'

Laszlo looked at her for one long, agonising moment.

'Really?' he said coolly. 'I wonder...' He ran his hand over the dark stubble grazing his chin. 'Just how badly do you want this job, Prudence? Are you prepared to beg for it?'

She felt nausea clutch at her stomach. 'You're a monster!' His eyes were cold and implacable.

'This is payback! Firing you makes us quits, *pireni*! And, believe me, you've got off lightly. If there were still wolves in Hungary I'd throw you to them. So if I were you I'd walk out of here while you still can.'

Prudence stared at him, her chest blazing with

anger. 'What does *that* mean? Are you threatening me?' she asked tightly.

Laszlo stared at her in silence, his eyes glittering with mockery. 'Threatening you? Of course not. But this discussion is over, so I think you should accept that and walk away.' His jaw tightened. 'That shouldn't be a problem for you. After all, you've had lots of practice.'

Anger swept through her. 'Oh, you think you're so clever, don't you? Well, let's get one thing clear. This discussion is *not* over.'

He gazed at her impassively in silence. Finally he said, almost mildly, 'Then I suppose you'd better start talking. Although I'm not quite sure what difference you think it will make.'

She stared at him in confusion. How did he *do* that? Only moments earlier his anger had been incandescent beneath his skin. Now he was prepared to grant her an audience. It was impossible to keep up with him. She gritted her teeth. But hadn't it always been this way between them, though? With her trying to chase the moods which ran like quicksilver through his veins?

She lifted her chin. But the blood was humming in her ears and she felt suddenly hot and stupid in the face of his cool composure. Was she just expected to somehow plead her case while he stood there like some hanging judge? Fixing her gaze on the wall behind him, she swallowed.

'I admit I made mistakes back then. But you're punishing me for them *now*. How is that reasonable or fair?' She paused and heat burnt her cheeks as he stared at her. For a moment his eyes fixed on her, as though her words had meant something to him, and then he shook his head slowly.

'Fair?' he echoed. '*Fair!* Since when did you care about fairness? You dumped me because you didn't want to live in some tatty trailer.' His eyes hardened. He, on the other hand, would have been content to sleep under the stars if she was with him. Shaking his head, he gave a humourless laugh. 'How was that fair to me?'

Blood colouring her cheeks and collarbone, Prudence flinched, his bitterness driving the breath from her lungs. It was true—she *had* said words to that effect—but she hadn't meant them, and whatever Laszlo might think, she'd been so madly in love then that she would have lived in a ditch with him if he'd asked.

All she'd wanted was for him to repudiate her fears that he'd lost interest in her or, worse, found someone else. Only he'd been so dismissive. And bored. As if she was a nagging child. So it had been impossible to tell him the truth, for that would have meant revealing the depth of her love. She'd been too upset to do that, but just angry enough to want to provoke him and hurt him for not loving her. And so instead she'd lashed out at him about the mess and the cold and the rain.

Prudence felt a trickle of misery run down her spine, but then, almost in the same moment, she shook her head, anger filling her. He was taking what she'd said out of context and—surprise, surprise—ignoring the part he'd played.

Damn it! Unlike her, he'd actually thought they were married! So why hadn't he done more to make it work between them? Did he think that relationships just sustained themselves? A lump formed in her throat. It certainly seemed that way. She'd gone to him for reassurance but he'd left her no choice but to walk away, and it had been the hardest choice she had ever made. Even talking about it now made her heart swell with grief.

She lifted her chin. 'We're not going to go there, Laszlo. I am not going to talk about the past with you any more.' Heart thumping, she took a breath. 'If you wanted to discuss our relationship you should have done so at the time. Frankly, now it's irrelevant.'

Her grip tightened on the chair as he stepped towards her. She felt her stomach swoop. Close up, his beauty was radiant and piercing—like a flaming arrow. His eyes were more golden, his skin smoother, the angles and shading of his cheekbones almost too perfect to be real.

'I don't agree. I think it's entirely relevant, given that you have brought our past back into my life.'

Her mouth trembled. 'That's not true, Laszlo. It was you who contacted Seymour's.'

She stared at him indignantly. If he hadn't wanted anything to do with her then why had he chosen to use her uncle's firm? Only of course he didn't *know* it was Edmund's business. He didn't even know her uncle's name, let alone what he did for a living. She shivered. Somehow now didn't seem like the best time to tell him.

Trying to ignore the pounding of her heart, she swallowed. 'I know how you hate being responsible for anything, but this is *your* mess.'

'And we both know how you hate mess, Prudence,' he said smoothly.

'I didn't care about the stupid trailer!' she snapped, her temper rising. 'You just focused on that and wouldn't listen to me. It wasn't a criticism of you, or your precious Willerby Westmorland! It's just who I am.' Her heart was thumping so hard it hurt. 'I don't like mess. I like things tidy and in order and that's why I'm good at my job. Maybe if you'd thought about that instead of sneering at me—'

'I'm not sneering, *pireni*.' His face shifted, and meeting her angry gaze, he shrugged. 'And you're right. Maybe I did focus on that remark—'

He stopped and Prudence gaped at him speech-lessly. Was that some kind of apology?

His eyes locked with hers and he sighed. 'But I'm not going to change my mind, Prudence. You do understand that, don't you?'

'Yes,' she said stiffly. 'But, given that it's prob-ably not just your decision to make, I've decided it doesn't matter.'

Laszlo frowned. 'You think there's a higher au-thority than me?'

His eyes gleamed with sudden amusement and she felt her stomach flip over.

'I hope so—for Mr de Zsadany's sake.' Wonder-ing again if Janos knew of her relationship with Laszlo, she felt a stab of pain. He was such a fraud.

Why, if he'd believed himself to be married, had he kept her existence secret?

Forcing herself to stay focused, she lifted her chin. 'Seymour's is the best there is. Giving this job to another firm would only demonstrate how unqualified you are to have anything to do with the cataloguing.' Hers eyes flashed challengingly at him. 'I mean, you don't even *like* art!'

'I appreciate beauty as much as the next man,' Laszlo said softly.

'Really?' Prudence retorted. 'How do you work that out? The only time we went to see an exhibition together you spent your entire time in the café.'

Laszlo shrugged, his gaze sweeping slowly over her face until heat suffused her skin.

'I can think of better things to do in a darkened room. You, of all people, should know that.'

Prudence stared at him, trembling, dry-mouthed; her body suddenly a mass of hot, aching need. He let the silence lengthen, let the tension rise between them.

'Or have you forgotten?' he murmured finally. 'Perhaps I should jog your memory.'

He watched her eyes widen and felt his groin

tighten in response. But almost immediately he closed his mind to the tormenting tug of hunger.

'But I digress. I don't need to like art, Prudence. I just want to support my grandfather and be there for him—'

'Good luck with that!' Prudence interrupted him crossly. '*Being there* for someone generally requires an element of reliability or commitment, you know.'

She glared at him as his gaze rested on her accusing face.

'Meaning...?' he asked slowly.

'Meaning that *you* can't commit to the next five minutes.' She stared at him incredulously. 'Don't you know yourself at all? Trying to pin you down to a time and place is like asking you to give up your soul or something.'

A slight upturn of amusement tugged at the corner of his mouth. 'Ah, but at least you admit I have a soul.'

And then suddenly he smiled, and it felt like the sun on her face. Despite her brain warning her not to, it was impossible not to smile back—for it was a glimpse of the Laszlo she had loved so very much. The Laszlo who, when he chose, had been able to make her laugh until she cried. But then her smile faded and she reminded herself that *this* Laszlo had cold-heartedly used his power to avenge himself, regardless of the consequences to her or her family.

She frowned. 'Life can't always be improvised. Sometimes you have to do boring things too—like learn lines and turn up on set on time.'

Laszlo stared at her, a muscle working in his jaw. 'You're comparing our relationship to a film?'

'Yes. I am.' Prudence lifted her chin. 'A very unmemorable silent film, with poor casting and no plot.'

She felt the hairs stand up on the back of her neck as he smiled again and shook his head slowly.

'I think your memory is playing tricks on you, *pireni*. There were some very memorable scenes in our film. Steamy too. Award-winning, even.'

'For the best short film?' she snapped.

'I was thinking more hair and make-up,' he said, his eyes glittering.

She couldn't resist. 'Yours or mine?'

'Oh, definitely mine,' he whipped back.

There was a silence, and then both of them started to laugh.

Prudence stopped and bit her lip. 'Can't we stop this—please, Laszlo?' She saw the indecision on his face and for a moment she faltered, and then she said quickly, 'It's brutal. And senseless. We're just going round and round in circles, and all this name-calling isn't going to change the fact that your grandfather wants his collection catalogued and I'm here to do it. So let me do it, Laszlo: for him. For your grandfather.'

Their eyes locked: hers bright and desperate, his, dark and unreadable. She swallowed hard, trying to find the words to change his mind.

'If I lose this contract you won't just be punishing me,' she said steadily. 'Other people will suffer—people you've never met…people who've done you no harm.'

She held her breath and watched his face, trying not to let her desperation show.

'Please, Laszlo. Please don't make this personal. Just let me do my job and then I'll be out of your life for ever.'

There was a tense, expectant silence as he studied her face. She wanted this job, badly, and he wondered idly just how far she would go to get it back. Immediately prickling heat surged through him and his groin grew painfully hard. He gritted his teeth, shocked by the intensity of his body's response.

It would be easy to give her a chance. His chest tightened painfully. But why should he? After all, she had never given their marriage a chance, had she? His face hardened. Did she really think that she could somehow emotionally blackmail him into forgetting the past and the harm she had done to him? And what about his family? What about *their* pain?

He remembered the long days and nights spent watching his grandmother's health fade, the years spent living with the guilt of not having given her the great-grandchildren she'd so longed for.

Prudence held her breath, watching a sort of angry bewilderment fill his eyes. The tightness around her heart eased a little: maybe all was not lost yet.

'Can't we just forgive and forget?' she said softly. He looked up and she hesitated. 'Please, Laszlo. I don't believe you really want to do this.'

His face was stiff with tension. Slowly he shook his head. 'Then you clearly don't know me at all, Prudence.' His mouth was set in a grim line. 'I *want* to let you stay. For my grandfather's sake, you understand. But I can't,' he said simply. 'You see, I'm half Kalderash Roma. We don't forget or forgive.'

He paused and his voice, when he spoke again, was like the sound of a tomb sealing.

'And you're still fired.'

Prudence gazed at him in shock, her ragged breathing punctuating the silence in the room. A sense of impotent despair filled her and then something else: a hot and acrid frustration that burnt her stomach to ash.

'I see. So it's not your choice.' Her hands curled into fists. 'How convenient for you to be able to blame your stubbornness and your spite on genetics.'

His narrowed gaze held hers. 'I'm not blaming genetics. I'm blaming *you*.'

'But not yourself?' She stared deep into his eyes. 'Nothing is ever your fault, is it, Laszlo?' she asked flatly. 'You just saunter through life, expecting everyone around you to take responsibility for the nasty, boring bits.' Smiling bitterly, she shook her head. 'I thought husbands and wives were supposed to give and take. Not in *our* marriage, though!'

She tensed as he stepped towards her, his eyes suddenly gleaming like wet metal.

'So now you're my wife? Interesting! As my charms clearly weren't sufficient to persuade you of that fact seven years ago, I can only imagine that my grandfather's wealth is a more compelling reason for you to belatedly acknowledge our marriage.'

Prudence glared at him. 'How dare you? I couldn't care less about your grandfather's wealth.'

'Just about my poverty?' he said bleakly.

'No!' Biting back the hundred and one caustic responses she might have made, she shook her head. 'This isn't about wealth or poverty. This is about what's happening here and now. About how you're prepared to make everyone suffer—me, Edmund and all the people who have worked so hard to make this happen.' She ticked them off on her fingers. 'All because you're so blinkered by your stupid male pride that won't see sense!'

'And you're so blinkered you couldn't see beyond my trailer to the people living inside,' snarled Laszlo.

'That's not true,' Prudence said hotly. 'If I didn't see those people it's because you would never introduce me to anyone.'

His eyes narrowed. 'You're such a hypocrite. You didn't want to be part of their lives any more than you really wanted to be part of mine.'

For a moment she didn't reply. It was true. She

hadn't wanted to be part of his life: she'd wanted to be all of it. As he'd been all of hers.

She shook her head. 'You don't know what I wanted.' She shivered on the inside. He never had.

Feeling suddenly close to tears, she clenched her fists, struggling to find a way past her misery.

'Fine! Have it your way! I was everything you say and worse,' she said flatly. 'That doesn't mean I'm not good at my job. But if you fire me you'll never know. Until you're stuck with a second-rate replacement.' She paused and shot him a challenging glance. '*If* you can find one, that is.'

'Oh, that shouldn't be a problem. I had no trouble replacing you last time,' he said softly. He watched the colour leave her face.

'I'm not surprised,' she said hotly. 'Being the grandson of a billionaire and owning a castle must have a lot of pulling power with a certain kind of woman.'

Watching his eyes narrow at her insult, she felt a flicker of triumph that blotted out the misery of his words.

'It's nice to know that you took your wedding vows so seriously,' she snapped. 'Having vilified *me* for not believing our marriage was real. Who's the hypocrite now?' Breathing deeply, she let her eyes meet his—steel clashing with bronze. 'We could stand here trading insults all night, Laszlo, but this isn't about our personal qualities. It's not even about us. There are other people involved. Not just people, but family. Just remember how anxious your grandfather was to get started. Don't his feelings count?'

She paused as, with a jolt, she suddenly realised that Mr de Zsadany was sort of her family too. Shock swept over her in waves. She stared at him, legs shaking, stomach plummeting. Suddenly she had to know for certain.

'Is that why he chose Seymour's?' she blurted out. 'Because he thinks I'm your wife?'

Laszlo stared at her calmly. 'No. He doesn't know we're married. No one does except my cousin and my great-uncle. I didn't see the point in upsetting everyone.' His eyes hardened to stone. 'Especially not my grandfather. He wasn't strong enough to deal with it.'

She felt dizzy, sick with wretchedness. 'I'm sorry. I really am.' It sounded so inadequate, even to her. 'But surely that makes this easier? My staying, I mean?'

She took a step back from the white heat of his anger.

'*Nothing* about you being here is easy.'

'I just meant—'

'I know what you meant,' he said bleakly. 'I know you better than you know yourself.'

Her misery gave way to fury. 'Stop being so sanctimonious. You've just spent the last half-hour telling me how contemptible I am for not believing in our marriage but you didn't even tell anyone about us.'

She glowered at him.

'You don't actually feel any more married than I do, do you, Laszlo? What's upsetting you is the fact that *I* didn't think our marriage was real.' Biting her lip, she pushed a strand of tousled blonde hair behind her ear. 'That's what this is really about. That's why you're punishing me. Not because you really care about our marriage. If you did then how could you treat me like this? I mean, do you honestly think that any *normal* man would fire his own wife?'

She flinched as he raised his eyebrows, his lips curling in disbelief and contempt.

'That would depend on the wife...' he said slowly.

He studied her face, noting the small frown between her eyes, the delicate flush colouring her cheeks. She was so disingenuous! His feelings about their marriage might not be consistent or rational, but at least he hadn't deleted its very existence. He frowned. He should hate her—and he did. And yet his body was responding to her just as it had done in the past.

She shook her head. 'You can't use our marriage against me, Laszlo. Married or not, you never really let me in.'

She swallowed. Except when they'd made love. But there was more to a relationship than just lovemaking. Like trust and honesty and a willingness to share.

Sighing, she shook her head. 'I get that your life was complicated. I even sort of see why you didn't tell me everything at the start. But nothing changed after we "married". You still kept me on the outside.'

She met his gaze, her hurt and anger clearly visible in her eyes.

He felt his chest tighten painfully. 'You didn't give me a chance. You barely managed to stay around long enough to digest the bread and salt we shared at our wedding. Besides, you're just talking about details.'

'Details?' Prudence stared at him incredulously.

'*Details!* Your grandfather is a billionaire and you call that a *detail.*'

She shook her head. She felt light-headed—almost dizzy. How could he stand there with that contemptuous look on his face as if he was the one who'd been tricked?

'You're unbelievable! You deceived me. And you kept on deceiving me.' Her voice sounded jagged. 'Not just about some tiny, stupid detail but about who you *were*. Don't you see how that makes me feel?' She stopped abruptly, like a train hitting the buffers.

Laszlo's face was cold and stone-like. 'I imagine it feels no worse than realising my background had some bearing on your feelings for me.'

The contempt in his eyes seemed to blister her skin.

'Besides, my grandfather's wealth is not pillow talk: I don't discuss the state of his finances with every woman I sleep with.' He gave a short laugh.

Prudence felt the room lurch as the implication of his words sank in. She clenched her hands together to stop them shaking.

'I wasn't "every woman". I was your wife. Or have you forgotten?'

He shook his head slowly. 'I try to forget every

day, *pireni*. One day I may finally do so. But, either way, I will never forgive you. And you're still fired.'

There was a frozen silence. Prudence could taste rust in her mouth—the corrosive tang of failure. Her body felt limp, spent, her mind reduced. She had no words left inside—or none that had the power to reach him anyway. It was over. And now that it was, all she wanted to do was get away from him as quickly as possible, with all that remained of her dignity.

'Fine. Then perhaps you could call me a taxi for the airport? I should like to leave as soon as possible.' Her head suddenly felt impossibly heavy, and she pressed her hand against her temple.

Laszlo watched her. Even though anger still festered inside him, he found himself reluctantly admiring her courage in defeat.

'If that's what you'd prefer,' he said.

His voice was that of a stranger: polite, solicitous, but remote. It pricked her like a needle and she felt a cold, creeping numbness begin to seep through her body at this poignant reminder of the irrevocable shift in their relationship.

'Our car is at your disposal, of course.'

Prudence shook her head. 'Thank you, but no

thank you,' she said stiffly. 'I'd be happier making my own way.' She hesitated and then, lifting her chin, said flatly, 'I don't know what you're going to say to your grandfather, but please would you pass on my apologies for what's happened? I really am sorry for any inconvenience this may have caused him. And I'm also sorry not to be meeting him. He sounds like a remarkable man.'

Pausing, she stared fixedly at a point above his head.

'And there's something else—' Noticing the irritation on his face, she shook her head. 'It won't take long.'

He nodded but suddenly she found she couldn't speak. She knew what she needed to say—she just wasn't certain of how to say it. She just knew that as long as she remained 'married' to him her life would never be her own.

Gritting her teeth, she drew a quick breath—for what more had she to lose?

'If I'd known you were here I never would have come. But…' She paused and took another breath. 'But I'm glad now that I did. Seeing you again has made me realise that I need to draw a line under what happened between us.'

Her face felt suddenly hot and dry and her unshed tears felt like a burden of lead. But she would not cry. Not until she was on that plane home.

Watching his eyes narrow, she smiled stiffly. 'Don't worry. I'm not going to go over it all again. Let's just agree that we were both too young and we made mistakes.' She hesitated. 'But we're older now, and wiser, and so we can put them right.'

'Put them right?' echoed Laszlo. His words were expressionless but there was a glimmer of emotion in the hammered gold of his eyes.

'Yes,' Prudence said flatly. She swallowed. 'I mean obviously neither of us wants to meet again. So I think we should take this opportunity to sort our relationship out once and for all.'

The air felt suddenly tight around her. Gasping, she lifted her chin and found herself on the receiving end of a bone-chilling stare.

'I see. So what exactly are you suggesting?' Laszlo said softly.

Prudence tensed. Whatever inner strength she had, it wasn't enough. Not nearly enough to dig a hole big enough to bury the past and the pain. And she was done with digging. She needed closure. Something formal. Something that would let her get on with her life. And now maybe she'd found it.

'Our marriage is over. We both accept that. All

I'm suggesting is that we make it official. I think we should get a divorce, however we do that.'

Her voice trailed off and there was a small, tight pause. Her cheeks felt hot.

Suddenly her heart was beating like a drum and she found herself babbling. 'It's been seven years, Laszlo. Our lives have moved on. We just need to tie up all the loose ends.'

It was the wrong thing to say. She watched his shoulders stiffen with a tension that thinned the air between them.

'Is that what I am?' he said, his gaze probing her face with such fierce intensity that suddenly she was holding her breath. 'A *loose end*?'

She ignored his question. 'I don't want this hanging over me. Without a divorce we'll both be trapped by something neither of us wants any more. I want my freedom.'

'*Freedom?*' Laszlo demanded.

She flushed. 'I want closure. I want to move on,' she said urgently.

'You want to move on…' Laszlo lifted his eyebrows. He looked at her impassively but there was a dangerous glint in his eyes.

'Stop repeating everything I say! Yes, I want to

move on.' Prudence jerked her chin up. 'I have a career now. And if I meet someone...'

Suddenly he was no longer coolly aloof but intent and alert.

'Did you have a particular someone in mind?'

He spoke softly—courteously, even—but there was no mistaking the hostility and challenge in his voice.

Prudence stared at him, transfixed. 'No. I don't. Not that it's any concern of yours.'

His eyes clashed with hers and she tensed in their glare.

'No concern of mine? And how do you come to that conclusion, *pireni*?'

'Easily,' she said irritably. 'We haven't seen or spoken to one another for seven years. We have no claim on each other whatsoever.'

Laszlo's eyes lifted to hers and with shock she saw passion and possession in their burnished depths. 'And yet here you are: my wife.'

Heat rose up round her neck, coiling tendrils over her face and throat.

Shaking her head, she took a small, hurried step back from the intensity of his eyes.

'You know what? Forget it! Let's just leave it to the lawyers.'

Her heart was thumping and her palms felt suddenly damp as he shook his head slowly.

'I don't believe in divorce.'

She stared at him in silence, her skin prickling beneath his gaze. 'So what are you saying?' Her voice rose. 'That we carry on as though none of this happened?' It was her turn to shake her head. 'Laszlo, that's *insane*! Why on earth would you want to do that? You don't even *like* me.' She paused, her colour rising betrayingly. 'And I certainly don't like *you*!'

'Is that right?'

He gave her an infuriating smile and she gritted her teeth together.

'Yes, it is. It's been a long time since I've been susceptible to your charms.'

Her pulse twitched at the lie and she had to clench her hands to stop them covering the tips of her breasts, which were pushing treacherously against the thin fabric of her blouse.

'Are you sure about that?' he whispered.

Transfixed, Prudence caught her breath. Her skin was taut and tingling, as though a storm was about to break, and as his eyes travelled questioningly over her trembling body she felt a slow, rippling swell of tension rise up inside her. He stepped towards her and her stomach plummeted. She knew she should protest, or push him away, and she opened her mouth. But no words came, for something in his gaze had drained the last atom of resistance from her.

'Let's just see, shall we?' he murmured softly.

Imprisoned by a hope, a longing she knew she should resist, she felt her body melt as he brought his lips down on hers with a fierce urgency. And then there was no one but him, his insistent mouth on hers, and a swimming giddiness tugging her down into darkness.

He tasted sweet and salty. And hot. Her eyelids fluttered and her mouth opened and then she was kissing him back greedily, her lips bruising against his. And all the time heat was climbing inside her, spiralling upwards. Frantically she squirmed against him, pressing her body to his, her hands tugging at his shirt, plucking clumsily at the buttons.

He kissed her hungrily, with lips that formed no words but spoke of danger and of something like belonging, and his kisses made her feel fearless and strong.

She heard him groan, and then abruptly he released his grip and stepped away. She opened her eyes and stared at him, confused, feeling a coldness against her skin where moments earlier she had felt the pressing warmth of his lips and fingers. Her body was trembling like a leaf in the rain and hastily she clutched at one of the armchairs for support.

There was a long, pulsing silence and then Laszlo shook his head and said quietly, 'Not susceptible?'

Prudence gazed at him, dazed; her brain felt fogged and her lips were tingling and tender from the heat of his kiss. She could hardly believe what had just happened—what she had let happen.

'We shouldn't have done that,' she said shakily. 'It was a mistake.' She took a step backwards, her eyes darting frantically around the room.

Laszlo studied her coolly. 'No. Our marriage was a mistake. That...' He stared mockingly at her swollen mouth. 'That was just a demonstration of how little you know yourself.'

Somewhere in the castle a clock began to chime and, frowning, Laszlo glanced at his watch. His face darkened and he shook his head, his mouth set in a grim line.

'It's too late now for you to catch a flight home.'

There was a tense silence and then finally, in

a voice that made her stomach turn in on itself, he spoke.

'You'll have to stay here tonight.'

He stared at her coolly, his eyes dark and implacable.

'But don't get any ideas. I'm only letting you stay out of the goodness of my heart.' His eyes glittered. 'Nothing's changed, Prudence. You have one night and one night only.'

She found herself holding her breath as he studied her face.

'After that I don't ever want to hear from you or see you again,' he warned softly. He studied her coldly. 'A word of advice, though. I wouldn't bother trying to pursue this matter outside of this room. The stakes are too high. It won't just be your pride that gets hurt.' He paused, his eyes fixed to her face. 'I'll ruin Seymour's too.'

In other words, she just had to accept her dismissal in silence. *Unfair dismissal,* her brain screamed. He couldn't just fire her like this.

Only he could. And he had.

Worse, there was nothing she could do about it. The De Zsadany Corporation was a huge, global company that had almost limitless funds and an entire publicity department at its disposal. She felt a shiver of apprehension. There was no doubt in her mind that if she tried to challenge Laszlo he'd use every weapon in his armoury to wipe not just her but Seymour's off the face of the earth.

It was bad enough that she was going to have to tell him that she'd lost the de Zsadany contract; she certainly wasn't going to do anything else to jeopardise Edmund's livelihood.

She shivered at the intensity in his expression as he spoke again.

'I don't suppose you'll want to hang about, so I'll arrange for a taxi to be waiting at…shall we say six-fifteen?'

Prudence nodded mutely.

'Good.' His mouth twisted into a grim smile. 'And make sure you're in it. Otherwise you, your family and all those nice people at Seymour's will live to regret it.'

And with that he turned and walked out of the room.

Her heart pounding erratically, Prudence stared after him. A rising hysteria was scrabbling inside her like a trapped animal. She'd ruined everything—and not just for Edmund.

She shivered. Seven years ago she'd vowed to forget him. Some mornings she'd barely been able to drag herself out of bed. Only one thought had kept her from pulling the duvet over her head: that in time she would be able to think of Laszlo Cziffra with nothing more than a bruised sadness. And one day she might just have managed it.

Her face quivered. One fervid, feverish kiss later and how foolish that hope seemed. For now she saw that it didn't really matter how much time she had. Seven years or seven hundred—it would make no difference. It would never be long enough for her to forget Laszlo and how he had made her feel.

Prudence lifted a hand to her mouth, remembering the burning heat of his kiss. How he could apparently still make her feel.

CHAPTER FOUR

LASZLO WOKE WITH a start. His room was dark and cold but it was not the cool night air which had shaken him from sleep. He shivered and rolled onto his side, feeling his heart drumming against his chest. It had been a long time since 'the dream' had woken him—so long he had almost forgotten the mixture of apprehension and panic that followed in its wake. Of course the feeling of dread would subside, but Prudence Elliot wasn't just haunting his dreams now. She was here, in his home, sleeping under his roof, her presence tugging at him like a fish hook.

Scowling, he rolled onto his back. In the darkness, he felt his cheeks grow warm.

Last night Prudence had accused him of being a coward and a liar. Her accusations—so unexpected, so bitter—had left him breathless; and now they lay lodged under his heart, cold and solid like stone. He rolled back onto his side, trying to shift the memory of her words, but the empty space beside him seemed only to strengthen their tenacity.

He felt misery swell in his chest.

Once upon a time he had imagined Prudence lying next to him in this very bed—had imagined bringing her to the castle as his new bride, even pictured her face, her surprise and excitement. He frowned. And now she was here. Only she was sleeping in a guest room and she had come not as his wife but as an unbidden, unwelcome intruder.

He grunted crossly. No matter. She would be gone soon enough. His breathing sounded suddenly harsh in the darkness, and anger, frustration and resentment fused in a rip tide of emotion.

Gritting his teeth, he shifted irritably beneath the sheets, knowing that sleep was inconceivable now. He fumbled in the darkness for the bedside lamp and a soft light illuminated the room. Squinting, he rolled onto his side. What the hell was wrong with him? Prudence's imminent departure should have comforted him, so why was the thought of it making him feel more tense?

He swallowed. Guilt. That was why. Picturing his grandfather's disappointment, he frowned through the ache in his chest. But what choice had he had? Working with her, living with her, would have been intolerable. Laszlo shivered, his jaw tightening. Firing her had been the right, the only thing to do. And it should have been the end of it. Only then she'd told him she wanted a divorce.

He winced inwardly: *divorce*. She'd thrown the word at him carelessly, almost as an afterthought. But to him it had felt like a punch to the head. Grimacing, he punched the pillow in return and lay back again. She had been so insistent—she who had never known her own mind, who had questioned every tiny detail. Demanding her freedom! Freedom from something she'd never even believed in.

The only thing that had mattered had been hurting her and proving her wrong, and so he'd kissed her. And, feeling her melt against him, he'd felt a surge of triumph. Only now the triumph had faded and he was lost—swept far away, a stranger to himself, his entire body a quivering mass of frustrated desire.

Damn her! He shouldn't be feeling like this; after all, he hated Prudence Elliot. A muscle flickered in his jaw and suddenly, remembering her mouth beneath his, his body instantly and painfully tightened. He rubbed his hands tiredly over his face. Okay: he wanted her. That was undeniable. Maybe *hatred* was the wrong word. It certainly didn't do justice to this whole set of feelings that were plaguing him now. Not that he even really knew what they were. Just that his life had grown infinitely more complicated and less certain overnight.

Abruptly he tired of his thoughts and hoping to shift the uneasy, shifting mass of arguments inside his head, he switched off the lamp and stared at the window, watching the light creep under the curtains. And then, feeling suddenly drained, he slid down under the bedclothes and sleep came at last as the sun began to warm his room.

It was time to leave.

Pressing herself into the corner of the taxi, Prudence sat back and, closing her eyes, said a silent farewell to Kastely Almasy. It should have been a relief to leave, to know that this was the end. But as the car accelerated down the drive she was fighting hard not to give in to the sense of failure and desolation that filled her chest. How could it have come to this?

Sadly, she remembered the first time she'd seen Laszlo. It had been at a funfair, and even though she'd been almost intoxicated by the lights and the noise, the screaming and too much sugar, she had still lost her footing when she'd noticed him standing slightly aloof from the crowd. His dark-eyed beauty had been like a shot of neat alcohol. A rushing, teasing dizziness she could still remember. In that moment, she had fallen swiftly and irrevocably in love and later lying in his arms, she had felt invincible in the sanctum of their intimacy.

Prudence sat up straighter, her jaw tightening. But that had been seven years ago. Now all that remained of that exhilaration and ecstasy was a crushing hangover. She sighed irritably. Tiredness was making her self-indulgent. Last night sleep had eluded her. Images from the evening, dark like wine, had spilled and spread through her dreams: Laszlo's brooding gaze, the sensual curve of his mouth, his strong hands reaching out to pull her closer…

Her body stilled as she remembered the fierce, vivid pleasure of his kiss and how badly she had wanted him to keep kissing her and touching her and—

Abruptly, her eyes opened. And what? She caught her breath. Wasn't letting him kiss her a big enough mistake? Perhaps she should sleep with him too, just to make her humiliation complete? Maybe then the message would get through to her.

That his kiss had been nothing to do with passion and everything to do with power.

She should have slapped him or pushed him away—or better still run away. But of course she'd done nothing of the sort. Her body had been utterly beyond her control—her hunger, her need for him, hot and unstoppable like lava. Even though he'd been so cruelly vindictive and unreasonable, everything and everyone—her family, her career, her pride—had been surrendered to the honeyed sweetness of his lips and the warm, treacherous pleasure gathering inside her.

Wincing, Prudence bit her lip. What had happened last night shouldn't have happened. But it wasn't surprising that it had. Last night their past had dropped into the present like an atom bomb. She and Laszlo had been like the survivors of a blast, staggering around, unable to speak or hear. Physical intimacy had been inevitable, for they had both been wounded and needing comfort. And besides, sex had always been the way they'd communicated best.

She stared bleakly out of the window, feeling the comet's tail of his caresses trailing over her skin, and then she shivered, feeling suddenly empty and drained. Now was not the time to be indulging in fantasies. Laszlo Cziffra might still be her 'husband' but he was not her lover. He was the enemy, and that kiss had been a ruthless demonstration of his power—not some resurrection of the passion they had once shared.

She lifted her chin, feeling anger effervesce inside her. How dare he twist what had been beautiful and blissful between them for his own ends! He was a monster! A bullying, manipulative monster. For all that talk of being married was just that: talk. After all, what kind of a husband would sack his own wife?

Seething with frustration, she glanced out of the window at the wall that edged the estate, her thoughts scampering in every direction. How could he just fire her anyway? She frowned. She, or rather Seymour's, had been hired by Mr Janos de Zsadany—not Laszlo Cziffra!

She felt another spasm of anger and then suddenly, unthinkingly, leant forward and hammered on the glass behind the taxi driver's head.

'Stop! Stop the car, please!'

She was out of the taxi before it had even ground to a halt and she caught a glimpse of the driver's startled face as she half stepped, half fell onto the road.

'S-sorry,' she stammered breathlessly. 'I didn't mean to scare you. It's just that I've realised there's something I need to do back at the castle.' She felt her cheeks burn as the man stared at her incredulously. 'I just remembered it. Just then,' she said hurriedly. 'So I'll just go back and…'

Her voice tailed off as he frowned and, suddenly remembering that she needed to pay, Prudence reached hastily into her handbag. But the driver shook his head.

'No. No need. It is settled. No need for money. But no need to walk. I take you back, yes?'

Prudence felt a sudden twinge of alarm. What exactly was she doing? And then, with shock and something like excitement, she realised that she didn't know—and what was more, she didn't care. All her life she'd made plans and followed the rules and what good had it done her?

She shook her head. 'No,' she said firmly. 'No, thank you. It's not far and I'll enjoy the walk. If you could just get my suitcase from the boot?'

She waited impatiently as the driver got out of the car and went round to the rear of the vehicle, releasing the boot to take out her case. He placed it beside her and she pulled up the handle and tilted the case back onto its wheels. She smiled her thanks at the driver and then turned and, heart thumping in her chest, began to walk back towards the castle.

Part of her expected to hear the driver call out, or turn the car round, but nothing happened and after a few moments she realised that for the first time since she'd agreed to go to Hungary she felt oddly calm—happy, even.

Finally she reached the tall iron gates. She stopped and drew a deep breath and, reaching out, pulled firmly on the handle. And pulled and pulled—and pulled again, and again, with increasing desperation. But it was no good: the metal creaked but the gates stayed obstinately shut.

For a moment Prudence stood pink-cheeked and panting, and then she let out a low moan. Of course—they were electric. She glanced wildly around for a bell but there wasn't one. There wasn't even a nameplate. How was she supposed to get back in?

She stared up and down the road but there was no sign of anyone, and finally she turned back to the gates, feeling her earlier bravado slip away. So that was that. Her one and only act of rebellion— over before it had even started. Looking up, she stared sadly at the stone wall.

Or was it?

Frowning, she glanced down at her high-heeled court shoes, and then in one swift movement she had kicked them off and tucked them firmly into her suitcase. Perfect! She took a couple of steps backwards and stared assessingly at the wall, and then, with as much strength as she could manage, she hurled her midsized case upwards. Holding her breath, she watched as it flew high into the air and over the top of the wall. It landed with a heavy thump on the other side.

Sighing in relief, she grabbed hold of one of the damp stones and began to pull herself up. It was easier than she'd thought it would be, and climbing down was easier still. She had just stepped back from the wall with a self-congratulatory smile when abruptly she felt a sudden rise in tension. The air stilled and her skin began to prickle. And then the breath seemed to ooze out of her lungs like a balloon deflating as she heard a familiar voice.

'Good morning, Miss Elliot! I'd like to say it's a pleasure to see you again but we both know that wouldn't be true, don't we?'

Prudence reluctantly turned round to find Laszlo watching her, his hands in his pockets, his face, as usual, unreadable. Dressed casually in jeans and a black polo shirt, his hair tousled, he looked younger, more carefree than he had done last night, but there was an intensity to his stillness that felt almost predatory to her.

'This dropping in on me is becoming a bit of a habit, isn't it? If I didn't know better I'd say you had designs on me,' he observed slowly. 'I must say that I'm a bit surprised—although perhaps *surprised* isn't the right word. *Shocked* might be better; or *outraged*—or perhaps *offended*. Given that you appear to be in the process of breaking into my home.'

Laszlo thrust his hands deeper into his pockets. Actually, as he'd watched her clamber down the wall he'd felt something closer to fear than anger—for what would have happened if she'd fallen and he hadn't been out walking the grounds?

Even though she was back on solid ground, Prudence felt her nerves scrabbling frantically for a footing. A sidelong glance at Laszlo did nothing to improve her composure: he seemed almost preternaturally calm. But there was no point in her having come back if she was going to let him intimidate her from the outset and, gritting her teeth, she held her head high and met his gaze defiantly.

Finally he shook his head and said lightly, 'So.

Did you come back to rob me? Or just to check that you'd finished me off with your suitcase?'

Prudence stared at him, her face white with shock. 'Of course I didn't come back to rob you!' She stopped speaking suddenly, momentarily confused. 'Wh—what do you mean, finish you off?'

Laszlo raised his eyebrows. 'What do I mean?' he repeated quietly, his expression cryptic. 'I mean I was taking an early-morning stroll, quite happily minding my own business, when suddenly I was nearly poleaxed by *that*.'

He glanced behind him and Prudence saw her suitcase lying on its side in the grass.

'That *is* yours, isn't it?'

She bit her lip and he watched her eyes darken, the black swallowing the grey, and then slowly she was smiling, and then she burst out laughing.

'I'm sorry,' she mumbled. 'It's not funny. I'm sorry—I really am.' She bit her lip again and tried to stifle a giggle as he shook his head, his eyes gleaming and golden beneath their dark lashes. And then, just as suddenly, his jaw tightened and it felt as if a bucket of cold water had been thrown into her face.

'It's a miracle you didn't injure someone. My grandfather often rises early and walks around the grounds.' He looked at her evenly. 'But I suppose no one was actually hurt, so I'll accept your apology. However, that doesn't explain why you're sneaking over my wall just minutes after I saw you leave in a taxi.'

Prudence felt her face turn hot with embarrassment and fury. 'I wasn't *sneaking*!' she snapped. 'I had to climb over the wall because the gates were locked.'

Again Laszlo raised an eyebrow.

'Indeed they are,' he said softly. 'They keep out unwanted visitors. Usually.'

Feeling clumsy under his cool scrutiny, but refusing to be intimidated, she turned to face him. 'I am *not* an unwanted visitor. I am here to do a job—a job I was hired to complete by your grandfather. You might want to send me packing but it's not your choice to make.'

Laszlo studied her impassively. He'd thought nothing could ever surprise him again after finding Prudence in his sitting room last night, but that was before he'd watched her scramble back into his life over a huge stone wall. And now she was refusing to leave unless his grandfather agreed to it.

Fingering his phone in his pocket, he looked away and gritted his teeth. It would be the work

of moments to call the taxi driver back and dou-
ble...triple his fare to take her away. So why was
he hesitating?

He glanced back at her and his groin tightened.
That was why! He felt heat slide over his skin and
wondered if she had any idea how incredibly sexy
she looked. Was this really the same shy girl he'd
married seven years ago? Standing there barefoot
on his lawn, her hair tumbling over her shoulders, her breasts thrust forward like a modern-
day Semiramis.

He shook his head, to clear it of this arousing,
unsettling chain of thought, and as if on cue she
stepped forward, eyes flashing, ready for battle.
'I won't leave on your say-so, Laszlo. You'll have
to drag me kicking and—'

'Okay. Okay.' He raised his hands in surrender.
'Give me your bag!'

Prudence looked up at him suspiciously. 'Wh—
why would I want to do that?'

Their eyes met and the silence between them
rose and fell in time to the sound of her heartbeat.

'So I can carry it for you. I don't usually conduct
business on the lawn. Let's go somewhere more
private. And safer!'

She heard the smile in his voice and, glancing up

at him, she felt her stomach flip over as his eyes locked on hers. 'Trust me. This lawn's actually much more dangerous than it looks.'

She felt the hairs rise on the back of her neck and suddenly breathing was a struggle. 'No, thanks,' she said hoarsely, averting her gaze. 'You probably just want to throw me in the moat or something.'

Laszlo shook his head and looked up at her speculatively through thick dark lashes.

'That definitely won't happen.' He paused, the corners of his mouth tugging upwards. 'We haven't had a moat since the sixteenth century.' Glancing up at the sky, he frowned. 'Besides, it's about to start raining. I'm too much of a gentleman to leave you to your one-woman protest, and rain means my hair is going to get wet. And you know what happens when my hair gets wet...'

Shaking her head, she gave a small reluctant smile. 'Gentleman? More like gentleman of the road!'

He winced as a drop of rain hit his shoulder. 'Come on, *pireni*! You know how much I hate it when my hair goes curly.'

Breathing unsteadily, her heart banging against her ribs, Prudence frowned.

'I promise I won't do anything you don't want me to,' he said lightly.

He watched the colour spread over her cheeks as she hesitated, and then she nodded. And then the clouds split apart and they ran as rain thundered down.

'This way!' he shouted over his shoulder as water splashed at them from every direction, and then, as one, they burst through a heavy close-boarded door into an enormous empty barn. 'We'll have to wait here until it stops!' He glanced down at her feet. 'Are you okay? You didn't cut yourself or anything?'

He had to yell to make himself heard and she shook her head dumbly. Was she okay? She was in a barn, alone, standing with a soaking wet, panting Laszlo. How was that ever going to be okay?

Her eyes fixed on his rain-spattered shirt, the definition of hard muscle clearly visible against the damp fabric. Instantly she felt a familiar tingling ache low within her pelvis: she knew exactly what lay beneath that shirt. She could feel a yearning deep inside for the ceaseless touch of his hands, his lips—

And then the air slammed out of her lungs as he suddenly shook his head like a dog.

Abruptly she heard the rain stop.

He looked up at her and Prudence felt her pulse jump.

'I don't want to have to drag your grandfather into this, Laszlo. I just want you to give me my job back,' she blurted out.

Laszlo studied her calmly. 'I know what you want,' he said slowly, and his shimmering golden gaze slipped over her skin in a way that made her stir restlessly inside.

Flustered, almost squirming with tension, she lifted her chin. 'Do you?' she said challengingly.

His eyes gleamed and the trace of a smile curved his lips for the briefest of moments—and then his smile faded. Staring at her broodingly, he let his gaze drift over her soft pink mouth and felt his body respond instantaneously. It had always been like this with Prudence—this fierce, relentless tug of physical need like a terrible, aching hunger that must be satisfied.

He frowned. He felt as if he was teetering on the brink of something.

'Okay,' he said softly. 'You can stay. The job is yours.'

Heart thumping, Prudence bit her lip. Had he really changed his mind? Or was this some sort of cruel game? But one look at his face told her that incredibly, unbelievably, he was telling the truth. She turned away to hide her confusion as instead of relief a spasm of doubt ran through her body.

'And you're sure about this?' she said slowly, looking up at him and frowning. 'Only it all seems a bit sudden. You changing your mind like this.'

Laszlo forced himself to meet her eyes. He was just going to have to hope that she accepted his volte-face as evidence of his impulsive nature. But the truth was that he was struggling to make sense of his decision too. 'You know me, Prudence. I can't resist a fork in the road. It's in my blood.'

Prudence stared at him suspiciously. She could hardly refute his claim; his mercurial moods and erratic behaviour had overshadowed their entire relationship. However, if this was going to be a business relationship, they needed to deal in fact. It didn't mean that he could try to fob her off with some flowery, meaningless nonsense.

'You're going to have to do better than that, Laszlo.' She shook her head. 'Why have you changed your mind?'

There was a loaded silence and then he shrugged. 'Seymour's are the best, and I want the best for my grandfather.' He surveyed her calmly. 'So, do we have a deal, then?'

She nodded slowly.

His smile tightened. 'But don't think that just because I've changed my mind anything has changed between *us*. I may be willing to forget the past for my grandfather's sake, but I haven't forgiven you.'

Nor was he entirely sure that he'd done the right thing, letting Prudence stay. But it would be for only a matter of weeks, and *he* would be calling the shots. Breathing out slowly, he felt a twinge of satisfaction—for now that he'd rationalised his behaviour, he saw that it would be immensely gratifying to have his beautiful English wife at his beck and call.

Staring defiantly at his face, Prudence clenched her fists, resentment curdling in her throat. She should be feeling relieved—ecstatic, even—for she'd fought to keep her job. But now the full consequences of having achieved that goal were starting to dawn on her and she felt more cornered than anything. He was in control here and she knew that. Worse—he did. And even worse than that was the knowledge that she still responded to the maleness of him with an eagerness that shocked her.

Her pulse leapt. Could she really do this? Work

and live with Laszlo? Remembering the heat of his lips on hers, she felt her body still and her breath snag in her throat. How could she still want him? After everything he'd done and said? It was incomprehensible. But while her heart might have hardened against him, her body still melted at his touch. Not liking that fact didn't make it any less true.

She turned to face him and found him watching her impassively. Looking away again, she swallowed. If ever she was weak and stupid enough even to *imagine* kissing him again, she'd need to remember that look—right there—to remind herself that Laszlo had coldly and without any compunction discarded her. No kiss and no caress, however sublime, could change that.

'I understand,' she said crisply.

It was on the tip of her tongue to say that receiving his forgiveness was not exactly top of her agenda, but she had no desire for yet another confrontation—and then she sucked in a breath as she realised that her inadequate instinct for self-preservation was the least of her worries.

'What about your grandfather?' she said abruptly. 'What are you going to tell him? About us?'

For a moment he said nothing, and she held her

breath, and then he turned to look at her, his eyes so golden and fierce it was like looking into the sun.

'What would you have me tell him? That I've deceived him for the last seven years?'

His voice seared her skin and she shook her head. He looked away, his mouth thinning to a grim line. She swallowed and took a stinging breath, hating herself but knowing that there was no avoiding it.

'And my contract?'

Laszlo studied her for a moment. 'Will be signed this morning. But until then shall we shake on it?'

Prudence stared at him in silence, her skin prickling. Taking a deep breath, she nodded and offered him her hand. His fingers brushed against hers, and then she gave a sharp cry of surprise as his hand slid over her wrist and he jerked her towards him, hard and fast, pulling her body close to his lean, muscular torso.

'Let me go,' she said, trying desperately to yank herself free.

She struggled against him but he simply drew her closer, clamping her body against his until he felt her resistance subside.

'No. Not until you and I have got a couple of things straight.'

Prudence gritted her teeth. 'Isn't that something to do when we sign the contract? You know—with a lawyer present.'

Her stomach flipped as she felt him weave his fingers through her hair, his hand holding her captive.

'You'll get your contract, Prudence. But we need to lay down a few ground rules just between the two of us.'

He tilted her face up towards him and her skin grew warm beneath his glimmering hypnotic gaze.

'Firstly, you're here to work. And whatever you might like to think, *I'm* your boss and I'll be working closely with you on this project. This is something my grandfather has asked me to oversee. So if you don't think you can stomach taking orders from me then I suggest you climb back over that wall right now.'

Clenching her hands into fists, she counted to fifty under her breath. Finally, after a long pause, she said stiffly, 'I understand.'

Their eyes met and he nodded.

'Good. Secondly, you will restrict your remarks to matters relating to the cataloguing. You will most certainly not discuss anything to do with our previous relationship or the existence of our marriage with anyone. And I don't just mean my grandfather.'

Prudence stared at him, her mouth trembling. 'Oh, don't worry—I don't intend to tell *anyone* about our marriage; it's not something I actually go around boasting about.'

His hand twisted in her hair and she squirmed in his grip as he jerked her closer. 'Finally,' he said softly. 'Something we can agree on.'

Her eyes slammed into his like thunderclouds colliding with the sun and then she shook her head wearily. She was beginning to wish that she'd just stayed in the taxi.

'You know what? I actually don't want to have anything to do with you when I'm not working. That's *my* ground rule. I came back for my job and that's what I'm going to do: my job. Not gossip about a marriage I didn't even know was real and that quite frankly was so long ago and so short I can't really remember it anyway!'

His eyes met hers and she held her breath, her blood humming in her veins.

'Oh, but I can,' he murmured.

His hand slid down her neck, cupping her chin, the thumb strumming her cheek, stroking slowly, steadily, until she arched helplessly against him, feeling his hard strength, his raw desire, and wanting more of both.

'I can remember every single moment.'

Prudence swallowed. She opened her mouth to speak, tried to lift her hands and push him away, but her brain and body refused to co-operate. Her head was spinning and she could feel her insides tightening, desire mingling with frustration and anger. And then he shifted against her so that the hard muscle of his thigh pushed against her pelvis.

She moaned softly, tipping her head back as his lips caressed her neck, moving slowly, deliberately over her throat and back to her mouth, and then her lips parted and he lowered his mouth to hers. Tingling currents of sensation snaked across her skin and, reaching up, she curled her fingers through his hair and drew him closer, gripping him tightly, for it felt almost as though she might disappear into the kiss itself.

And then, slowly at first, and then with a jolt, her brain seemed to awaken from a deep sleep and she broke free of his arms.

The air on her skin felt sudden and sharp, like a knife, and she rubbed her hand against her mouth as though to remove all traces of his dark, compelling kiss.

'We shouldn't have done that.'

Her voice was raw, her breathing coming in panicky little gasps. It had been wrong. And stupid and dangerous. A shudder ran through her. But how could it be wrong when it had felt so good and so right?

Laszlo watched her shake her head, a fierce, urgent heat flaring in his belly. He wanted her so much he could hardly stand. And she had wanted him—she still did. He could see that in the dark turbulence in her eyes and in the convulsive trembling of her skin.

'What are you talking about?' His voice was taut, his breathing fraying apart as he spoke.

'I don't want that—I don't want you—' she began.

Laszlo cut her off incredulously. '*That* was you not wanting me?'

Biting her lip, she shook her head, too horrified by the violence of her response to him even to try to dissemble her desire for him. 'No. I *do* want you.' Shivering, she took a step backwards, staring at him with wide-eyed agitation. 'But we can't. It would be wrong—' She looked frantically past him, trying to locate the door in the gloom of the barn.

Laszlo frowned. 'Wrong? How could it be wrong? We're married—'

It was her turn to look incredulous. 'It's not about whether we're *married*, Laszlo!' She shook her head again. 'It's not appropriate, our doing that, when—' She was struggling for words. 'I mean, you hate me.'

'I don't hate you,' he said slowly, and he was surprised to find that it was true. He didn't.

There was a shocked silence and she met his gaze.

'But you don't like me, and I don't like you, and we certainly don't love one another.' Her voice sounded wooden but her breathing was calmer now and she lifted her chin. 'This is just sex.'

'This is *not* just sex,' he said, speaking with slow, clear emphasis. 'You clearly haven't had much in the way of sexual experience if you think *that* was just sex.'

Her face coloured. 'You're right. I haven't. But when I make love to someone it will be because I love them and *only* because I love them. Not because of anything else.'

Knowing just how good that 'anything else' could feel, she clenched her fists against the treacherous warmth seeping over her skin.

'So, no, Laszlo. I'm not going to have sex with you in a barn even though we may be married.'

Crossing her arms in front of her body, she stared at him defiantly.

Laszlo studied her in silence. Had he really thought she would sleep with him? And would he have respected her if she had? He smiled grimly. Would he have respected *himself*? After all, he'd kissed her twice in twenty-four hours, each time telling himself it was the last time—each time, telling himself it was a mistake, that whatever desire he felt was just some reflex kicking in…a habit from the past. But why, if that were true, did he want to keep on repeating those mistakes? And go on repeating them.

He felt his body stir again and frowned. His mistake had been to believe he was over her—for he saw now that, like a virus in his blood, his longing for her had simply lain dormant until she'd walked back into his life yesterday and turned him inside out.

His jaw tightened. He needed some way to cure himself of this sexual power she had over him. Only he was so wound up he was finding it hard to think. All he knew was that his body was pulsing with frustration.

'Okay,' he said finally. He watched her breathe out. 'Look. We've both had a lot to take in. And we're still coming to terms with—' he waved his hand towards the roof of the barn '—everything. So I think we should cut ourselves a bit of slack. How about we go up to the castle and have some breakfast?'

Prudence nodded wordlessly. Her brain was in overdrive. Why had she said she 'might' be married to Laszlo? And why did the thought of being his wife make her stomach turn over and over in helpless response to him? Her mouth tightened. It was foolish and distracting. Even if she accepted his version of events, it was still not something of which she needed to be reminded. Particularly as she seemed determined to give in to the intense sexual chemistry between them at every opportunity.

Pushing back her shoulders, she reached behind her neck and smoothed her hair into a ponytail. Her body clearly had very poor judgement when it came to men and she would need to be on her guard at all times—otherwise this arrangement simply wouldn't work. And that was what she was here to do: work. Not concoct some parallel life in which she and Laszlo were happily married.

She realised that he had spoken again. 'Sorry—what did you say?'

He stared at her speculatively. 'I said that I'll introduce you to my grandfather after breakfast. And then we can sort out where you're going to sleep. It shouldn't be a problem. We have twenty bedrooms at the castle. Eighteen spare, that is.'

His groin tightened painfully as an image of her lying naked beside him in his bed slid into his head and he took a deep breath. Maybe their sleeping under the same roof was not such a good idea after all. Not unless he was prepared to sleep standing upright under a cold shower.

Prudence was clearly having the same thought.

'Why don't I just stay in a hotel?' she said quickly.

'That won't be necessary.'

A muscle flickered in his cheek. There was another option—only up until that moment the mere thought of suggesting it would have appalled him. But nothing was the same any more. Looking up at Prudence, he cleared his throat. 'There's an empty cottage on the estate. It's small. But it's clean and private and a lot cosier than the castle.'

His eyes blazed.

'Just don't get *too* cosy! As soon as the cataloguing is complete I want you out of my life and I never want to see you again.'

CHAPTER FIVE

'AND THIS IS one of my favourite pieces in the entire collection!' Janos de Zsadany took a step back and stared intently at the portrait of a girl clutching an open green fan. 'Annuska and I gave this to Zsofia for her sixteenth birthday.' He turned towards Prudence and gave the faintest of smiles. 'I think secretly she'd been hoping for a horse. But thankfully she was enchanted.'

Prudence gazed at the portrait. 'It's beautiful!' she said slowly. 'Were you specifically looking for a Henri?'

Janos shook his head. 'No. Not at all. But when Annuska and I saw this painting we both knew it was the one. She reminded us so much of Zsofia. Not just in colouring. It's her expression.' He smiled ruefully. 'My daughter often used to look at me like that. You know—that mixture of love and exasperation.'

Prudence bit her lip. She had suddenly realised that they weren't talking about some random young woman but Laszlo's mother. 'I'm sure it was just her age,' she said hesitantly.

She felt suddenly sick with guilt. Janos was talking so openly about such a private matter with the woman who was secretly married to his grandson. But what choice did she have? She sighed. It had been easy enough to agree with Laszlo not to discuss their marriage with anyone. It was not even that hard to convince herself that it was all for the best. Only now, faced with Janos's gentle courtesy, their subterfuge made her feel shabby and sly.

She sucked in a breath and managed a polite smile. 'Whatever your reasons, it was a good choice, Mr de Zsadany.'

Janos laughed. 'I think so too.' He beamed at her. 'I think we're going to get along very well, Miss Elliot.' He frowned. 'But could I suggest we do away with all these formalities, or we'll spend most of our time together repeating each other's names. Please call me Janos!'

Smiling, she shook his hand. 'Prudence,' she said firmly. 'And thank you, Janos, for making me feel so welcome.'

He bowed. 'No. Thank *you* for making this happen. You've made an old man very happy. And, as sorry as I am that Seymour was unable to be here, I'm in no way disappointed by his replacement. Don't worry, though! I won't tell anyone. It can be our little secret.'

'A remote castle in Hungary and a beautiful woman with a secret. How intriguing! It sounds like the plot for some kind of historical romance.'

They both turned to find Laszlo watching them from the doorway. His eyes fixed on Prudence and then his gaze shifted to his grandfather, his face softening into a smile.

'So!' He walked into the room and stopped in front of the painting, frowning. 'What's the big secret, then?'

He was still smiling, but his voice was blunt— like a knife against a whetstone. Since her arrival he'd been tormented by dreams of Prudence naked in the barn, and yet every time he'd met her she'd been polite but glacially remote. His smile tightened. It was an icy aloofness that appeared to be reserved only for him, for she'd established a sweetly flirtatious rapport with his grandfather.

Shaking his head, Janos patted his grandson on the arm. 'Oh, I was just trying to reassure Prudence that her presence here was in no way a disappointment. In fact, I'm rather hoping she might agree to be a charming, if sadly temporary, addition to our bachelor evenings of chess and back-gammon.'

Forcing herself to look straight ahead, Prudence managed a faint smile. 'That would be lovely, Mr de—I mean Janos. But I wouldn't want to intrude.'

Janos shook his head. 'Not at all. You're a long way from home,' he said firmly. 'And while you're our guest it's our job to make you feel welcome—isn't it, Laszlo?'

Prudence caught her breath as Laszlo gave the ghost of a smile and nodded slowly. 'Of course, Papi,' he said stiffly. 'But right now you need to go downstairs and find Rosa. Apparently you're supposed to be discussing curtains?'

Janos frowned. 'Ah, yes. The curtains. I hadn't forgotten. I just rather hoped Rosa had.' He ran a hand over his face and cast an apologetic glance towards Prudence. 'If you'll excuse me, my dear? Perhaps, however, I can persuade you to join Laszlo and myself for lunch?'

Watching Janos leave, Prudence felt a pit open up in her stomach and the air seemed suddenly to swell in the pulsing, steepening silence. Since arriving at the castle three days ago she'd made a point of staying in the cottage outside of work hours, and had hardly seen Laszlo except at meal-

times, when she'd found his marked courtesy towards her both grating and depressing. Only now
here they were: alone. There was nowhere to hide
from his dark, probing gaze. Or from the fluttering, shivery anticipation squirming inside her.

Biting her lip, she reached up to tuck her hair
behind her ear before remembering that, as usual
for work, she'd tied it back into a low ponytail.

'I don't have to come to lunch. I could say I
have work to do. Or that I've got a headache.' She
spoke quickly, desperate to say something before
her body began to slip apart and she couldn't even
think straight, far less talk.

Laszlo stared at her, his face expressionless, and
then he said coldly, 'I'd rather you didn't keep lying
to my grandfather, Prudence.'

She glared at him. 'I'm not lying. I *do* have work
I could be doing.' And, turning, she began to rifle
pointedly through a pile of papers on the desk.

'And the headache?' Laszlo said relentlessly.

Gritting her teeth, Prudence turned back to face
him. 'Also true—and standing right in front of
me!' she snapped.

Laszlo stared at her for a long, long moment,
until finally he began to drift around the room.
From the corner of her eye, she watched furtively

as he walked up to his mother's painting and idly ran a finger down the frame.

'Don't you have somewhere to be?' she snapped finally.

Turning, he shrugged, and then in a voice that made the hairs on the back of her neck stand upright, he said mildly, 'I have a cure for headaches.'

His eyes locked onto hers and she felt heat break out on her skin. Clenching her fists, she gave him an icy glare. 'So do I. Painkillers. In my handbag.'

Laszlo frowned. 'You shouldn't take pills for a headache. They're not a cure. You need to treat the cause, not the symptom.'

Prudence glanced at him irritably. 'I'm sorry, I didn't know you were a doctor. Is that another of your parallel lives?'

A muscle flickered in his cheek. 'I don't like you taking drugs.'

'It's a painkiller!' she said through gritted teeth. 'And I'd be grateful if you kept your remarks to matters relating to the cataloguing. That is unless you think my drug-taking is affecting my job—'

She gazed at him in astonishment as he began peering under tables and rifling through canvases. 'Be careful! Don't touch them without gloves.'

She hurried across the room, and then her feet stuttered to a halt as he turned to face her.

'Wh—what are you doing?' she stammered. His eyes rested on her face and, legs shaking, she pressed her knees together as her body tightened automatically in response.

'I'm looking for your high horse,' he said softly. 'Or is he in stables with all the others?'

Prudence swallowed. 'Very funny! I don't know why you're making fun of me. It was you who said we couldn't discuss anything apart from the cataloguing. I'm just following the rules.'

'But I make the rules. And I can change them too.'

She held her breath as his eyes locked onto hers. Then, abruptly, he walked towards the window and glanced outside.

'What you need is some fresh air,' he said smoothly. 'And some sunlight. A walk, maybe. You used to like going for walks.'

Prudence licked her lips. A sudden, all too vivid memory of where a walk with Laszlo might lead flashed into her head and she felt heat rise up inside her. Cheeks burning, she fumbled for the remnants of her anger—for something that would banish the slow, treacherous thickening of her blood.

'Okay. I'll go for a walk before lunch. Satisfied? And now, if you don't mind, I have work to do.'

Desperate for him to be gone, she put her hands on her hips and stared pointedly at the door. But instead of leaving he simply stood and watched her in silence until she thought she would scream.

'Why are you still here?' she snapped finally. 'Don't you have some suits of armour you could polish or something? I thought you had a job running a restaurant.'

He shrugged, shook his head. 'A chain of restaurants actually. But no. I'm entirely unoccupied.'

Her eyes narrowed. In other words, he was bored. And she was—what? The entertainment? 'Well, I'm not,' she said flatly. 'So why don't you go climb your towers and survey your estate?'

'Turrets…' Laszlo murmured. 'From the Italian *torretta*. They help protect a castle from hostile intruders. At least, they're supposed to.' He raised an eyebrow. 'I'm ready when you are,' he added softly.

Prudence felt a niggle of dread. 'Ready for what?'

He frowned. 'Our walk, of course.'

His eyes were fixed on her shocked face and she shook her head. Her heart was suddenly pounding so hard she could hardly hear herself.

'I said no, Laszlo!'

She took a step back and Laszlo stared at her mockingly.

'Come on! You need some fresh air. And besides, Rosa gave me some linen to bring over to the cottage. I'll never hear the end of it if I let you carry it. So either I can come with you now or I can drop by later.'

Prudence stared at him in silence; she felt like a mouse cornered by a cat. But surely she was being over-anxious? She glanced down at her demure navy blouse and olive-coloured work trousers. It wasn't as though she was dressed for seduction. Besides—she bit her lip—she didn't want him turning up at the cottage at night!

'Fine. Let's get it over and done with, then. But I'll need to take one of these boxes back with me, so you'll have to wait until I've sorted out the paperwork.'

Five minutes later she was walking resentfully towards the cottage, trying to ignore the fact that Laszlo was strolling alongside her, clutching what appeared to be nothing more burdensome than a pile of tea towels. To add insult to injury, the document box she'd chosen to bring with her seemed to have doubled in weight since they'd left the castle and her arms now felt as if they were on fire.

'Here. Let me.' A lean brown hand reached out towards her.

'I can manage,' she muttered, but Laszlo ignored her feeble resistance. Tugging the box out of her hands, he tucked it under his arm before continuing to saunter calmly by her side.

Determinedly she carried on walking, staring fixedly at the horizon until finally, and to her infinite relief, she saw the roof of the cottage come into view.

She stopped and turned towards him.

'Thanks very much. I think I can take it from here.' Looking up at him, she blinked, feeling suddenly hot and stupid as he smiled at her coolly.

'You know, it's hotter than I thought,' he murmured, glancing up at the midday sun. 'Perhaps I could just grab a glass of water?'

She caught the glint in his eye and gritted her teeth; he'd be asking for a pot of tea and biscuits next. Quickening her pace, she marched across the grass, fuming in silence.

Suddenly he was beside her again. 'Why aren't you talking?'

Eyes flashing with fury, she spun round to face him. 'Mainly because I have absolutely nothing to say to you.'

She watched the corner of his mouth tug upwards.

'Oh, I think you've got plenty to say to me,' he said softly.

Feeling hopelessly out of her depth, she let out a breath and pointedly looked in the other direction.

Laszlo watched her intently. 'Perhaps you're right,' he murmured. 'I've always thought talking was overrated and I can think of much better things to do with your mouth.'

Her chest grew tight. Things were getting too complicated. Breathing was suddenly difficult, and hastily she began to walk down the sloping path that led towards the cottage. The path was still damp from some overnight rain, and as her shoes slithered beneath her she almost fell. Her heart jerked as Laszlo reached over and caught her hand to steady her.

'Careful,' he warned softly. 'Or is walking with me so traumatic you'd rather break your own neck?'

Knocked off balance by the unexpected gentleness in his eyes, she stood half swaying against him. Her blood was singing and heat and confusion crackled under her skin. Looking up, she saw that the sky had grown dark. The air felt suddenly viscous and heavy. A storm was coming.

'It's these shoes. The soles are slippery,' she mumbled, her cheeks suddenly hot.

'Don't worry. I've got you,' he said calmly.

Holding her breath, she felt his grip on her hand tighten as the first drops of rain splashed onto her face.

They ran towards the cottage, stopping at the door to face one another.

'I guess I don't need that water any more,' he said hoarsely.

Heart pounding, Prudence stared at him. She knew he was giving her a choice. But what choice was there really? Wordlessly she stepped towards him and then, by way of reply, she reached up, slid her arm around his neck and pressed a desperate kiss against his mouth.

Groaning, he pulled her against him, pushing the door open with his body and kicking it shut behind them both. Her mouth parted beneath his and he pulled her towards him, capturing her face between his hands. Grunting, he pulled lightly at the knot at the nape of her neck, tugging her hair free, weaving his fingers between the silken strands.

She moaned, curling her fingers into his shirt, and he deepened the kiss, slowly, languidly sliding his tongue between her lips, teasing her, tasting heat and sweetness. He felt her stir restlessly against him and he groaned softly, his groin tightening in response as she kissed him back, pressing her mouth to his, then catching his lower lip between her teeth.

Senses swimming, he lifted his mouth, his breath snagging in his throat as her hands slid under his shirt, and then he turned his head, breaking the kiss. His pulse seemed to trip and stumble as the scent of her, warm and clean and sweet, filled his nostrils.

'Prudence...' he murmured softly. She looked up at him and his stomach clenched, his body growing painfully hard. He saw the struggle within her eyes that so sharply echoed his own. 'Don't be afraid. I won't hurt you.'

The tension inside him was fast, dark and swirling, like a spring tide rising. He could barely breathe for wanting her. Suddenly he was fighting to stay calm.

Reaching out, he touched her cheek gently. 'Do you want this?' he asked roughly. The air felt suddenly thick in his throat and he could barely speak. 'Do you want me?'

She looked up at him and their eyes met, and

then she nodded, and her face seemed suddenly to open and uncurl like a flower feeling the sun.

Slowly he let out his breath, and as he traced his thumb over the soft fullness of her mouth, he heard her gasp. A fierce heat engulfed him, for it was the sound of surrender. Desire leapt in his throat and, leaning forward, he lowered his head, brushing his lips over hers.

'I want to see you. All of you,' he whispered hoarsely.

In the darkness of the room her eyes looked feverish, almost glazed, and her soft pink mouth was trembling. Reaching out, he undid the fastening of her trousers and gently pushed them down over her hips. Straightening up, he watched dry-mouthed as she unbuttoned her blouse with trembling hands and shrugged it off, so that she was undressed except for the palest pink bra and panties.

Time slowed and Laszlo gazed at her, heart thudding, wordless, waiting. Heat seemed to burn every inch of him and his head was spinning wildly.

'Take them off,' he said finally, and slowly she unhooked the bra and peeled it from her shoulders.

His breath rasped in his throat as he stared at her small upturned breasts. She was so beautiful. Helplessly, he reached out and pulled her towards him, sliding his hands slowly up her thighs, over her hips and waist to her breasts, his thumbs brushing against them until he heard her cry out in pleasure.

Then suddenly, he was guiding her back towards the sofa, tugging his shirt off at the same time, wanting to feel the touch of her skin against his. Breathing deeply, he wrenched off his shirt. His eyes never leaving her face, he moved swiftly towards her, straddling her legs and pressing his mouth against the petal-smooth softness of her throat, then lower to the curve of her breast. His lips grazed the rose-coloured nipple, feeling it quiver and harden, and then his mouth closed over the tip, his tongue sliding over it, taking his time.

Blood was roaring in his head, swelling and rolling, humming like a cloud of bees about to swarm. Blindly he reached out and cupped her bottom, lifting her against him. He heard her gasp, felt her arch closer as his hands moved slowly over her hips and between her thighs. He felt her still beneath him as his hand caressed the apex of her thighs, brushing over the already damp silk. Gently he slid her panties over the curve of her bottom. Her fingers gripped the muscles of his arm and she whispered his name, and then her hand moved down over his chest and stomach and she was tugging at the buckle of his belt.

He groaned as she unzipped him, her fingers curling around him, freeing him. Trembling, his breath quickening in his throat, he shifted his weight, moving between her knees, spreading her legs. Her hips lifted to meet him and he pushed up, entering her with a gasp. He heard her answering moan of pleasure and began to move, thrusting inside her.

She clutched him tighter, her body shuddering, her hands tangling through his hair, pressing against him, pressing and pressing—and then she tensed and he heard her cry out. As he felt her flower beneath him he thrust hard, his muscles rippling, his breath choking in his throat and his body spilling inside her.

He lay still and spent. Her body was still gripping him tightly, and gently he caressed her warm, damp skin, feeling the spasms of her body fade. The sound of the rain was deafening now and he was grateful, for it blotted out the frantic beating of his heart.

Breathing unsteadily, he buried his face in her neck, trying to sort out his thoughts. It had been inevitable, he told himself bleakly. Since that moment in the barn the sexual tension between them had been ratcheted up to breaking point. Every single time they'd met it had felt like a minor earthquake. And today, finally, they'd snapped. His heart began to beat faster. It was only natural.

He frowned. But that didn't make it right. He glanced down at the woman lying in his arms. In the barn, he had ached with wanting her. Her refusal to give in to the powerful sexual attraction they had for one another had been infuriating, not to say painful. He sighed. But now he wondered whether by giving in to that hunger he'd merely set himself up for another sort of discomfort.

His breathing slowed. Hypothetically, it was easy to fall into bed with a woman to whom you had no commitment. There was no need for post-coital conversation or affection. No need even to see her again. But Prudence wasn't just any woman. She was his wife and pretty much nothing about their relationship was easy.

Feeling her shift against him, he frowned. Now he'd added another layer of complexity to their already tangled relationship. In fact, he was struggling to work out how to even describe what was going on between them—for while he was ostensibly her husband, he was also her boss…and now her lover.

Lightly, he traced a finger down her arm. He must have been crazy to let her stay and work for him, and crazier still to end up sleeping with her. But how was he supposed to resist her when everywhere he looked she was there? Laughing with his grandfather or bending over a notebook, her bottom jutting so alluringly towards him… His face darkened as he felt her stir beside him. It was too late to worry about resisting her. The only question that remained was what he should do next.

Shifting his weight slightly, he turned his head and stared down into her face.

Prudence looked up at him in silence. Her head was still spinning but she didn't want to speak anyway. For to speak would be to break the spell. Drifting her fingers over the flat muscles of his stomach, she bit her lip. It had felt so good—too good, she thought, heat colouring her cheeks as she remembered the sharp intensity of her climax. But then, making love with Laszlo had always been shockingly exciting. It was hardly surprising that her body still responded to him so fiercely.

She felt a twinge of alarm. Hardly surprising, but

not particularly sensible. Her eyes closed. There was nowhere to hide from what she'd done.

She'd made love with Laszlo. A man who had broken her heart seven years ago and made her feel worthless and stupid. A man who, she'd since found out, had lied to her for the entire length of their relationship but who held her responsible for ending their affair. Her eyes opened. Oh, if that wasn't messy enough, he was both her boss and apparently her husband too.

She shivered and, frowning, he pulled her against the warmth of his chest.

'You're not cold, are you?'

She managed a weak smile. 'No. I was just listening to the storm. I think it's moving off.'

Laszlo reached out and cupped her chin with his other hand. 'It's not, you know. It's right here. In this room. Can't you feel it?'

His fingers began to drift languidly over her stomach and lower, to the triangle of soft curls at the top of her thighs. She knew she should push him away, tell him to stop, but already she could feel her pulse quicken in response.

'We need to get dressed,' she whispered quickly, for soon she wouldn't be able to speak or think or even be aware of anything except the ruthless seeking rhythm of his caresses. 'For lunch.'

His fingers stilled and then she felt a sharp tug, like a fish hook in her stomach, as his warm palm slid over her breast, pulling gently at the nipple until she felt soft and hot and aching inside.

'I can't wait that long,' he murmured, catching her hand and pushing it down towards his groin. 'I'm too hungry.'

Without giving her a chance to reply he lifted her hips and drew her against him, his mouth stifling her soft gasp of excitement. And even though something deep inside her knew she was heading for disaster she arched herself willingly against him as the fierce heat swept over her again.

CHAPTER SIX

GLANCING UP AT the window, Prudence frowned as a few small drops of rain hit the glass. Mr de Zsadany—she still thought of him as that privately—had given her the afternoon off and she'd been hoping to walk into the nearby village. Now that plan would have to wait. She sighed. Not that it mattered really; she had a stack of books by her bed or she could even just watch some old black and white movie on TV.

She bit her lip. Only that would mean going back to the cottage. Her face flared, as it did every time she remembered that scene inside the living room: she and Laszlo, their bodies fused together, moving effortlessly against and inside each other, outside of time and reality. Her happiness had been absolute—and for the first time in such a long while she had felt savagely alive.

Only now, back in reality, she had to face facts. She'd simply picked up from where she'd left off seven years ago. Only at least then they'd actually been in love—or she had. And to Laszlo, at least, she had been—her mind shrank from the words—his wife.

Crossly, she snatched up a pile of papers and stuffed them without her usual care into a file. Now she was nothing more than a fool and a clichéd fool at that. She shook her head. The castle might be a romantic setting but the truth was more prosaic: she'd just slept with her boss. Like some naive heroine in a lurid story, she'd allowed herself to be swept away by a tide of fate and co-incidence. And lust!

She blinked. What was *wrong* with her? She had practically *invited* him to have sex with her. Her stomach clenched and she felt a pang of queasiness. How *could* she? Knowing what she knew about him and how he felt about her. For someone who'd vowed never to fall for his charms again, she'd certainly fallen into his arms with almost embarrassing alacrity.

Biting her lip, she picked up a paperweight and thumped it down on top of a pile of certificates. Who was she trying to kid? What had happened between her and Laszlo had been inevitable. But also horribly confusing. Lying in his arms had felt so natural, so familiar—as if she still belonged to him. And afterwards, when he'd pulled her against him, kissing her passionately right up until the moment before he'd calmly ushered her into lunch, that too had felt as if it meant something.

She frowned. But it hadn't. What they'd shared had just been sex. And after seven years of occasional dates and virtual celibacy, what she'd been feeling had simply been loneliness and lust. Only it had been impossible for her to see that, because intimacy with Laszlo shouldered out all rational thought.

She sighed. It was too late for regrets. All she could do now was keep her distance. Which shouldn't be hard, given that shortly after she'd let him take what he wanted he'd simply disappeared, slipping away like a swallow at the end of summer.

Picking up a box of files, she glanced round the empty room dispiritedly and sighed. Wouldn't it be wonderful if she could make her longing for him disappear just as easily?

An hour later, hair newly washed and dressed in a faded sundress, she wandered slowly around the garden behind the cottage. She felt slightly calmer now, restored by the fresh air and the sunlight. The rain had stopped, the sky was a clear blue and a light wind brushed her bare legs as she crossed the lawn.

With a cry of pleasure she spotted a cherry tree and, after pulling down a handful of the gleaming dark fruit, she bit into one. It was perfectly ripe and a sharp sweetness filled her mouth.

And that was when she saw him, walking slowly towards her across the grass.

It was all she could do to keep breathing. She stood, tracking him with her eyes, until he stopped in front of her. There was a roaring sound in her ears and her pulse scampered like a mouse across the floor as his gaze met hers—golden, steady and unwavering.

'I've been looking for you,' he said quietly.

Skin prickling, she stared at him in silence, hardly able to believe it was him.

'It's my afternoon off,' she said finally, glancing at him and then quickly looking away. 'Can't it wait until tomorrow? I'll be back at work then.' The gentlest of breezes caught her hair and, suddenly conscious of his focus, she felt her face grow warm.

'It's not work-related,' he said softly.

Their eyes locked and Prudence flushed. 'Then we have nothing to discuss.'

He laughed softly. 'In other words, we have a lot to discuss. Let me guess: you're mad at me for going off like that?' He lifted his hands in a gesture of surrender. 'I'm sorry I disappeared. I had to be somewhere. But if it's any consolation I've been thinking about what happened a lot.'

Prudence stared at him in silence. 'Did something happen?' she said slowly, trying to affect an air of nonchalance. 'I didn't notice. Just like I didn't notice that you'd disappeared.'

A slow smile spread across his face and then, shaking his head, he reached out towards her. Her heart contracted. It would have been so easy to give in, to let him take her into his arms, to lean in to his warmth and strength. But instead she raised her hands, curling them into fists.

'Don't!' she said fiercely. 'Don't even think about it! Honestly, Laszlo. You're unbelievable. Did you really just think you could roll up after two days and expect to carry on like before?'

His eyes narrowed. 'I said I was sorry. What more can I say?'

She stared at him helplessly. 'What *less* could you say? You didn't even say goodbye. But don't worry, I'll say it for you now. Goodbye.'

She turned to walk away but he reached out and grabbed her arm.

'Let go of me!' Jerking her wrist, she tried to pull herself free, but he merely tightened his grip.

'I'm sorry, okay?'

Shaking her head, she tugged herself free of his hand. 'It's *not* okay. How could it ever be okay?' She grimaced. 'Laszlo. We broke the rules.'

'I'm aware of that. But I don't see why you're getting so upset about it. We're both consenting adults.'

Gritting her teeth, she took a step towards him. 'It's not that simple.'

His face stilled and her skin seemed to catch fire beneath his gaze.

'Oh, but it was. Simple and sublime.'

She caught her breath, achingly aware of just how sublime it had been. How sublime it had always been. For a moment she hovered between desire and anger, and then anger won.

'It's not simple and you know it. It's a mess,' she snapped.

He studied her dispassionately. He hadn't intended to argue with her. On the contrary, he'd been looking forward to seeing her again despite the fact that she was right: it *was* a mess. He smiled grimly. After they'd made love he'd held her in his arms, trying to rationalise his behaviour, and on some levels it had been easy to explain. It was perfectly natural for any man to be attracted to any woman—and what man wouldn't be attracted to Prudence? She was beautiful and clever and poised.

His face tightened. Only then he'd started to think about their marriage, and about lying to his grandfather, and suddenly he'd wanted to be free of the tangled mess of his thoughts. A flush coloured his cheeks. And so he'd simply walked out, fully intending to stay away until the cataloguing was complete. Only after just two nights he'd changed his mind, driven back to the castle by a sudden inexplicable need to see her smile.

She wasn't smiling now. Her face was taut and strained, and he knew that his sudden disappearance had angered and hurt her. *Hell!* Why couldn't she just accept his apology and move on?

He stared at her coldly, his dark hair falling across his forehead. 'What do you want me to say, Prudence? I thought you enjoyed it. I certainly did.'

She was staring at him as though he were speaking in Mandarin.

'This isn't about whether I *enjoyed* it or not.'

'Then you really don't know yourself at all, Prudence. You slept with me for the same reason I slept with you. Because what we have is incredible. Physically, we couldn't be better matched.'

Prudence blushed, heat seeping over her throat and collarbone. There was a loaded silence.

'Fine. I agree,' she admitted finally. 'But that doesn't change the fact that our doing what we did makes everything so much more difficult. Even you must see that.' She stared at him agitatedly. 'I can't believe you just *left*. That you didn't think we should at least have one tiny conversation about it.'

He shrugged and glanced across the lawn, his gaze drifting away towards the horizon. 'What's there to talk about?'

'Everything!' she cried. 'You. Me. Us. My job. Our marriage. Where do you want to start?'

He stared at her, his golden eyes reflecting the early-afternoon sun. 'At the beginning.' He gave her an infuriating smile. 'When we got married. Which makes you my wife.'

She gazed at him helplessly. 'Only I don't feel like your wife, Laszlo! It still doesn't feel like a real marriage to me. But even if it did we haven't been together for seven years. We broke up—remember? And now we've crossed a line.' She bit her tongue. 'I know couples who split up do end up sleeping together and it's understandable. I mean, everything's so familiar and safe and easy.'

Feeling his steady gaze on her, she paused, blushing, for none of those adjectives bore any relation to her intimacy with Laszlo.

She glowered at him. 'But they have a one-night stand! They don't have to live and work with each other afterwards. We do—and I don't even know how to describe our relationship any more, let alone how to make it work.' She felt a spurt of anger. 'Everything's so messy and confusing, and you just stand there and do nothing like it's all going to just fall into place—'

'And what are *you* doing, *pireni*?' he interrupted her harshly. 'I fail to see what you think you're actually achieving here. You're just asking me unanswerable questions.' His mouth twisted. 'What happened between us in the cottage isn't the problem, Prudence. *You* are. You turn everything into an inquisition. Hell, seven years ago you turned our relationship into an inquisition.'

Prudence choked in disbelief. 'An *inquisition*? Did you ever stop and think *why* I asked all those questions?' She shook her head, bunching her hands into fists. 'No. Of course not. Our relationship was never about me, was it? It was only ever about you and your needs.'

Misery washed over her in waves and she curled her fingers into the palms of her hands to distract herself from the pain.

'I asked questions because I wanted answers. I wanted to know you; to understand you. But you made me feel like I was an intruder in your life. When you were there you never wanted to talk and then you'd disappear for days and I wouldn't know where you were. And you just expected me to put up with it.'

Laszlo shook his head in frustration. 'Not this again. You knew I didn't have a nine-to-five job. You knew I sometimes worked away for days at a time. And you knew I'd be back.'

'No, I didn't.' Her voice sounded suddenly loud and harsh. 'I *didn't* know that.'

Her whole body was shaking and she stopped, breaking off as she saw from his face just how baffling and irritating he found her insecurities. She bit her lip. She'd had reason to feel like that. Only aged twenty-one she had felt too unsure of his love, too aware of how boring he found any sort of soul-searching, to blurt out her life story.

'I didn't know,' she said again, more quietly this

time, for the old pain was welling up, making her hurt inside.

'Meaning what, exactly?'

His face was like stone and she looked away from it. 'I know it sounds crazy but I *didn't* know that you'd come back. Every time you disappeared I thought that was it. And I couldn't bear it.'

Laszlo said nothing and she felt the pain inside her spread. But had she really thought he would want to understand now, after seven years of hating her, just because they'd had sex again?

'Why did you feel like that?'

His voice was so gentle it startled her, and she looked up, half thinking that someone else must have asked the question.

'Did you feel like it right from the start?'

She nodded slowly, suddenly deprived of speech. Looking up, she saw him frown.

'But if you felt like that,' he said softly, 'then why did you stay with me?'

Prudence sighed. There in that one sentence was why their relationship had ended. For surely he knew the answer to that—just one look at her face had been enough for her Uncle Edmund to guess the truth.

She'd stayed because she'd fallen deeply and desperately in love with him.

Those few short weeks with him had been the most incredible, the most exciting time in her life. Exciting but terrifying, for Laszlo had unlocked a part of herself that she'd denied and feared in equal measure: a part of herself that she'd spent most of her life trying to repudiate or forget.

And here, now, after everything they'd done and said, she was afraid of giving too much away. Or, worse, destroying the memory of their time together, the time when she'd loved him and believed he loved her. Her lip quivered. She might no longer love Laszlo, but part of her still wanted to protect and preserve her memories.

'Like I said, I was acting a little crazy.' She smiled weakly.

Laszlo studied her. 'You were never crazy. Anxious and insistent, yes. And sweet, gentle and sexy.' His gaze rested on her mouth. 'Not crazy, though.' He paused, his eyes cool and unreadable. 'But why does that mean you didn't think I'd come back. I mean, I admit I was unreliable. But I was *reliably* unreliable: I always came back.'

He was attempting a joke and she tried to smile.

But instead, to her horror, she felt hot tears sting her eyes and she shook her head.

Laszlo stared at her with a sort of bewildered anger and then his jaw tightened. 'So you're saying it's my fault? I made you feel like that?'

But Prudence didn't answer; she couldn't. Not with Laszlo standing so close. He wouldn't understand her fear, the creeping uncertainty. He was just so certain of himself—so sure and utterly without doubt.

'Please. Tell me. I want to know,' he said slowly.

Some roughness in his voice made her lift her head. And then, after a moment, he reached out and touched her hand, uncurling it with his fingers.

'I might even be able to help.'

Heart pounding, she took a deep breath. 'It wasn't you.' She gave him another weak smile. 'Although you didn't help much.' Her heart twisted. 'It was me. I was just waiting for it to happen. Waiting for you to leave and not come back. Like everyone else.'

She felt close to tears again, remembering the waiting, fearing, hoping that it would be different—

'Who's everyone else?' Laszlo frowned, his face darkening. 'You mean other men?'

Prudence laughed. 'What other men? There haven't been any. Not really since us—and certainly not before.' She shook her head, frowning. 'No. I mean my mum—and it's a long story. You won't want to hear it.'

Laszlo stared at her intently. 'I do want to hear it. Tell me about your mum.'

His face was focused on hers, the golden eyes calm and dispassionate and yet warm like the sun. She let out a long breath.

'My mum met my dad when she was nineteen. They got married and had me. And then he left her.' Her mouth trembled. 'He came back, though. He always came back after a bit. While he was away she'd be frantic, and sometimes she'd go out looking for him.' The skin on her face felt suddenly scorched. 'Or for someone who'd make her forget him. She'd leave me. On my own. For hours. Sometimes all night. I hated it, being alone in the house in the dark.'

She swallowed, lowering her gaze.

'I always knew when she was going to go out. And I'd try and stop her. Stall her by asking questions.' She bit her lip; her questions to Laszlo seven years ago had stemmed from the same fear. Letting out a long breath, she shrugged. 'She nearly always went out, though. Then one day my dad never came back. Just cleared out their bank account and disappeared. It turned out that he was married already—to two other women. So really they weren't even married,' she said flatly.

'And you thought I'd do that to you?' Laszlo's voice was neutral but his mouth was set in a grim line.

Prudence couldn't meet his eyes. 'I suppose, deep down, I did. I assumed the worst.'

And that was why she'd walked away. Because she'd been scared. Scared that the worst was already happening, and that if she stayed her life would settle, like her mother's, into a pattern of rows and pleading and disappearances and lies.

Looking up, she met his gaze and they stood staring at one another, the silence between them broken only by the humming of the bees and the faint sound of a tractor on the breeze.

'I didn't give you much reason to hope for the best, did I?' Laszlo said softly.

He scanned her face, seeing what he'd failed to see before: a young woman seeking reassurance. Not once had he stopped and thought to ask himself *why* she had been so anxious. Instead he'd convinced himself that her constant need for reassurance had demonstrated a feebleness of character unbecoming in his wife.

Reaching out, he pushed an unsteady hand through her hair and pulled her gently towards him. For a moment he imagined burying his face against the doe-soft smoothness of her neck, but then he frowned.

'You were my wife. I should have known these things about you. And the fact that I didn't is my fault,' he said slowly. 'But you're right. You *did* assume the worst. Only I'm not your dad.' She stiffened at his words and he grimaced. 'And you're not your mum, Prudence! From what you've just told me, she doesn't sound like the sort of maddeningly stubborn woman who'd climb over a massive wall to demand her job back.'

Blushing at that image of herself, she looked up at him. He smiled at her slowly, his eyes glittering with an emotion she didn't recognise.

'I wasn't that stubborn until I met you,' she said carefully, her grey eyes issuing him with a challenge.

Watching the colour return to her cheeks, Laszlo felt a flicker of admiration rise inside him. She was brave. Braver than he'd thought. Braver than himself. He knew just how hard it was to reveal the truth about yourself to anyone.

Loosening a strand of her hair, Laszlo curled it round his finger. If only they could go back to bed, so she could curl her body around his as she'd done at the cottage.

As though she could read his mind, she looked up and sighed.

'So what are we going to do? You said you'd been thinking about us a lot?'

They were back where they'd started. He frowned. 'Not us. It. About *it*. The sex.'

Her shoulders felt leaden and she was suddenly more tired than she had ever been in her life.

'Of course. My mistake!' she said wearily. 'I seem to be making a lot of those. Look, Laszlo. What happened between us isn't going to happen again. I don't want to sleep with you—'

'Yes, you do,' Laszlo interrupted her, his voice sharp and sure like a scalpel. 'You want me as much as I want you. And until you stop torturing yourself about that it won't stop, whether you're in London or in Hungary, married to me or not. You told me you wanted a divorce so you could move on. But you didn't even know we were married. Now that's *crazy*, Prudence.'

A muscle tightened in his cheek.

'I agree. We need to move on but what's holding us back is not some vows we made. It's this thing we have. This incredible need for one another. I'll "divorce" you, if that's what you want. But you need to accept that no piece of paper, or whatever it is you're hoping to get, is going to bring you physical closure.'

Prudence felt herself frown. What he was saying made sense. Being unaware of her marital status hadn't stopped the memory of him casting a shadow over her sexual relations with other men. A light blush spread over her skin. Their touches, their kisses, had seemed like insipid, inferior copies of the fierce, primal passion she had shared with Laszlo. But how was she ever to move on if she couldn't stop this burning want she had inside her for him?

She shook her head. 'I don't understand. Are you saying you *do* want a divorce?'

His eyes darkened. 'The divorce is irrelevant. You have to face the truth. We want each other. And that want is holding us back from living freely.'

'What are you suggesting?' she asked slowly.

He studied her face. The air was suddenly thick between them.

'I think we should keep on sleeping together,' he said softly. 'The truth is we both want to. And maybe that's what we need to do to get each other out of our systems for good.'

She stared at him, stunned into silence not just by his words but by her body's instantaneous response to them.

Finally, she shook her head again. It wasn't worth the risk. 'So your solution to this mess is to make our lives more complicated? What happened at the cottage was understandable—'

'It was incredible,' he corrected.

Ignoring his comment, and the traitorous heat rising up inside her, she forced herself to concentrate. *'Understandable,'* she repeated firmly. 'But it was spontaneous. A one-off. What you're suggesting would be deliberate and repeated. We can't do that.'

'It's nothing we haven't done before.' He spoke quietly but his eyes were fierce.

She blinked. 'No. Laszlo. *I* haven't done this before. Had an affair with my estranged husband, who doesn't even like me and also happens to be my boss! It's just wrong on so many levels.'

His gaze flickered over her face and he smiled a smile that lit up his eyes like the sun, spreading radiance and warmth over her.

He shook his head, his eyes glittering. 'No. What we share could never be wrong, Prudence,' he said softly. 'I agree, it's not a conventional arrangement, but what we have is so extraordinary, so overwhelming. Look, I don't know if it'll work, but when I'm holding you in my arms it feels like we know everything about each other. It's like our own perfect private communion.'

Gazing up into his face, Prudence felt herself wavering. She knew she should turn him down but the pull of his words was so powerful. She could no more resist him than the tide could resist the tug of the moon.

Laszlo let out a breath. His heart was pounding. Looking down, he saw with surprise that his hands were shaking and he wondered why. He gritted his teeth. It was frustration, he told himself. Two days spent thinking about Prudence's delectable body and his own body was hovering on the edge of meltdown. Particularly with her standing so close, looking so desirable.

And she was so very beautiful. Her eyes were shimmering like beaten silver and he could smell the sweet honeyed fragrance that clung to her skin and hair. But truthfully it wasn't just about her beauty. It wasn't even about the sex. Her bright enthusiasm for art, her doggedness in getting back her job, her sweetness with his grandfather—all charmed him, delighted him.

'It's not just the physical,' he said finally. 'I like spending time with you.'

Prudence swallowed. Her grey eyes flashed with reproach. 'Only when it suits you.'

Seeing the indecision in her eyes, he was on the verge of simplifying everything by pulling her into his arms and melting her resistance with the heat of his kisses. But something held him back—some confused idea that this was not the moment for passion.

Besides, he had something better in mind.

CHAPTER SEVEN

'COME WITH ME. I have something I want to show you.'

He held out his hand and after a moment Prudence took it. They walked slowly together over the rough, springy grass until finally they reached a copse of stunted, low-branched trees and he stopped and gently disengaged his hand.

'What are we doing?' she asked.

'We're meeting him here,' he said, turning to face her.

'Meeting who? Where? We're in the middle of a field.'

Grinning, he shook his head. 'We're meeting my cousin. And this is not a field. It's an apple orchard. My apple orchard,' he said softly, taking her hand in his again. 'A long time ago the estate used to make all its own cider.'

Biting her lip, she looked at him nervously. 'Your cousin? Won't that be a little awkward? I mean, he knows we're married...'

Her voice sounded shrill and shaky and, frowning, Laszlo pulled her towards him.

'Take it easy. I have about thirty cousins. This is a different one.' Gently, he pushed a strand of hair behind her ear. 'This is my cousin Mihaly.' He paused and studied her face speculatively. 'He doesn't know we're married. Only my great-uncle and my cousin Matyas know.'

He grimaced.

'And they're not here. Not that they'd say anything to anybody anyway,' he said slowly. 'I promise. You'd have more luck having a conversation with Besnik than you would at getting a word out of either of them.'

Squeezing her hand, he squinted into the horizon. 'There he is.'

He lifted his arm and waved at the outline of a man riding on horseback.

'That's Mihaly.'

Feeling somewhat calmer, Prudence let out a breath as he raised his hand to greet his cousin.

'Mihaly! How are you?'

Smiling shyly, Prudence turned to where Laszlo was waving and then gasped softly. Not at the dark-haired man sliding off the bare back of a sleepy-eyed white cob, but at the caravan behind the horse.

'Oh. That is so beautiful,' she whispered. 'Is that a *vardo*?' Blushing, she glanced at Laszlo and he nodded slowly.

He dropped her hand and walked swiftly towards his cousin. The men hugged one another and then Laszlo turned. Reaching towards Prudence, he tugged her forward by the hand.

'Mihaly, this is Prudence. She's working for my grandfather. Prudence—my cousin Mihaly. He's like a brother to me and he's a good friend. Just don't let him sing to you.'

Mihaly grinned and inclined his head. 'And don't let *him* play a guitar.' He winced. 'I'm still having trouble in this ear. And now, cousin, where do you want me to put this—because I need to be getting back.' He turned towards Prudence and grinned sheepishly. 'My wife is having our fifth child any time now, so I need to get home as soon as possible.'

After much manoeuvring, Laszlo and Mihaly finally managed to guide the *vardo* between the apple trees and across the fields to the cottage. Having detached the shafts from the pulling harness, Mihaly waved cheerfully and rode away.

Prudence stared at the *vardo* in wonder. 'When I was a little girl I had a storybook with a picture of a *vardo* in it. But I've never been this close to one before,' she murmured.

'Take a look inside.' Laszlo gestured towards the *vardo*. 'There's a bed and a dresser and a stove.'

Prudence climbed up the steps and then trod lightly inside the *vardo*. It was just perfect, with intricately painted roses and castles and bright embroidered cushions. She swallowed and climbed back down.

There was a moment's silence and then Laszlo said quietly, 'So, what do you think?'

His voice sounded hesitant and, glancing across, Prudence saw that his expression was strained—anxious, almost. Guiltily she remembered how he'd accused her of shunning his family. Clearly he wanted to know what she thought of his cousin.

She smiled. 'He seemed nice.'

Laszlo laughed. 'Not Mihaly! The *vardo*. Do you really like it or are you just being polite?' He stared at her, his gaze intent, a line of doubt on his forehead.

'N-no, of course I'm not just being polite,' she stammered. 'It's beautiful. Really. You're very lucky,' she said teasingly. 'A castle *and* a *vardo*! That's just plain greedy.'

He grinned, and then his expression shifted,

grew serious. He looked at her levelly. 'Actually, the *vardo* isn't mine. I've just been holding on to it for someone.'

She held her breath, sensing a tightness in him—a sort of eagerness. 'Whose is it?' she whispered. But even before he could reply she already knew the answer to her question. 'Is it mine?' she asked hesitantly.

He nodded, watching as her look of shock and confusion turned to happiness. 'It was supposed to be my wedding gift to you.'

He hadn't planned on telling her that the *vardo* was hers. He'd simply wanted to show it to her, for he'd known that it would soften her. A woman would have to have a heart of stone not to be ensnared by the romanticism of a real gypsy caravan.

She turned to smile at him and he smiled back. But his smile was hollow, for seeing her genuine pleasure made him feel shabby and manipulative and he felt a stab of jealousy. With shock, he realised that he wanted to *share* in her happiness. That he actually *liked* making her happy.

A muscle flickered in his jaw. 'It's more of a curio than anything. We wouldn't have lived in it, obviously—'

'Why not?' She frowned, instantly defensive.

'It's beautiful and romantic and it's got everything you need—'

'Everything but a toilet and a shower and hot running water.' He smiled ruefully. 'Give me a Willerby Westmorland any day!' His eyes gleamed. He watched her with mild amusement. 'And there's nothing romantic about not being able to wash,' he added drily.

'Why did Mihaly have it?' She glanced up at him tentatively.

His eyes met hers. 'He and my uncle restore *vardos*. They've been holding on to it for me.'

He paused and Prudence felt her face grow warm.

'That's where I went the other day,' he said softly. 'After I ran away. I went to my uncle's and I remembered it was there. Only I couldn't bring it back because one of the wheels was damaged. So Mihaly said he'd bring it over to me today.' His golden eyes moved over her face like the sun. 'I wanted you to see it before you leave,' he added calmly.

His matter-of-fact tone went some way towards taking the bite from his words but Prudence still heard the blood rush inside her head and felt her stomach clench as she came crashing down to earth. But of course she was going to leave. Her contract wasn't permanent and Laszlo had just agreed to divorce her. So why did she feel so cold? As though she'd suddenly stepped into the shadows?

Pushing that troublesome question away, she took a step towards the *vardo*.

'Is it really mine?' She turned to face him. 'I mean, could I spend the night here?'

He took so long to answer that she thought he hadn't heard her, but then he stared at her, his eyes impossibly gold and translucent, like clear new honey, and nodded. She hesitated, suddenly tongue-tied and blushing.

'I mean, with you.'

The words caught in her throat and the air felt suddenly charged around them. Their eyes locked and then slowly he walked towards her. Sliding his hands through her hair, he tipped her face to his.

'Me? Stay in your caravan?' Frowning, he pretended to think. 'Are you sure? I don't know. That sounds complicated,' he whispered.

She pulled away from him and held out her hand. 'Then I think we should keep things simple,' she murmured. 'Stick with what we do best.'

And then, taking his fingers in hers, she began to lead him up the steps into the *vardo*.

Prudence woke to the sound of birdsong. The *vardo* was warm with sunlight and for a moment she lay sleepily on her back, revelling in the ache of her body. Then, rolling over, she reached out and touched the space beside her in the bed. The sheets were still warm and, closing her eyes, she breathed in Laszlo's clean, salty, masculine smell.

In the last few days when they'd been together every private moment had been spent in bed. And every night Prudence lost count of the number of times they made love. At first, despite lack of sleep, she hadn't wanted the morning to come, for fear that daylight would break the spell between them. But on waking that first morning, without any apparent effort on their part, everything had fallen quite naturally into place, and now their days and nights had slipped into a pattern.

Most mornings Laszlo would wake long before she did—often before dawn. Sometimes he would get up and dress and return, waking her with breakfast. Other times he would reach out for her in the darkness, pressing her body against his, the beat of his blood in time to her heart…

At the memory of the way his mouth sought out hers, of his hands so gentle, yet demanding, she felt a familiar ache deep inside her pelvis that made her press her legs together. Blushing, she gave a squirm of pleasure. The sex was so good, and his desire for her was so intoxicating, so quick, so urgent—like pollen bursting from a flower. He made her feel so alive, utterly unlike herself. Lost in him she became passionate, brave and wanton.

She bit her lip. But soon it would be over. She would be back in England and back to a life without passion; a life without Laszlo. Slowly she rolled out of bed and sat up straight. A hard knot was forming in her stomach. She had spent the last week living in the moment, trying not to think, and more particularly trying not to think about the future. Easy at first, with the days and nights stretching out ahead of her, to do just that. Easy, too, to accept the rationale for what they were doing and ignore the fact that physical intimacy encouraged the senses to play all kinds of stupid, dangerous tricks on the mind.

Sighing, she lay back down and rolled onto her side. She had no one to blame but herself, for Laszlo had never offered anything other than sex. In fact, he couldn't have made it clearer that their affair was simply a finite means to an end—a way for both of them to find sexual closure. But being with Laszlo seemed to be doing little to reduce her hunger for him. Instead the hours she spent in his company seemed only to remind her why she'd fallen in love with him seven years ago.

'I don't normally like talking about work over lunch...' Janos paused and glanced apologetically around the dining room table. 'But I just wondered, Prudence, how you think the cataloguing is going?'

Prudence frowned and put down her fork. It was a perfectly reasonable question, but there was a tension in the old man's voice that made her hesitate and, looking across at him, she felt a ripple of concern when she saw that he looked drawn and tired.

'It's early days,' she said slowly. 'But we are making progress.'

Looking across at his grandfather, Laszlo frowned. 'You look a bit pale, Papi. Are you feeling all right?'

Janos shook his head. 'I'm fine, Laci. I'm just being a silly old man.'

Laszlo frowned. 'I doubt that,' he said firmly.

'What's up? Is something worrying you about the cataloguing?'

The old man shook his head. 'It's nothing, really. It's just that it all seems to be taking so much longer than I expected.'

Prudence felt her chest squeeze tight with guilt. All she'd been thinking about for the last few days was Laszlo; everything else—Edmund, England and even the cataloguing—had been pushed to the periphery of her mind.

'Please don't worry, Janos,' she said quickly. 'I should have warned you. This part is always incredibly slow-moving. There's always lots of gaps in the paperwork.'

'Particularly when a collection is owned by a forgetful old fool who can't remember what he bought or when and where he bought it?' Janos said slowly.

Prudence shook her head. 'Not at all. You'd be surprised how many people own art that's worth thousands of pounds—hundreds of thousands of pounds—and yet have no paperwork at all.'

'They need Prudence to come to their rescue,' Janos said, his smile returning.

Laszlo leant back in his chair, his face impassive. 'They can't have her. She's ours!'

His eyes gleamed with an intensity that made her lose the thread of what she was saying and she felt her skin turn to liquid.

Resisting the tug of his gaze, she cleared her throat. 'I'm sorry you've been worried. I know it can be a bit overwhelming...' She hesitated. 'I don't know how you feel about this, but I'm sure Edmund would be a good person to talk to about it.'

Janos nodded slowly. 'Certainly, my dear—if you think he'd be happy to give me an opinion?'

Grimacing, she laughed. 'Knowing Edmund, I'm sure he'll be more than happy!' She bit her lip. 'I don't always like what my uncle has to say, but maddeningly he's quite often right.'

Her words were simply meant to reassure Janos but, feeling a prickle of heat on her skin, she looked up and found Laszlo watching her.

'Is that so?' he said flatly. 'Your *uncle* is a man of many talents!'

His eyes locked onto hers and her heart began to pound, for she saw that while his face was still and calm, his eyes were alive with anger.

'How *fortunate* for all of us,' he said slowly.

Laszlo felt a sickening wave of nausea. His

stomach twisted. Edmund Seymour was Prudence's *uncle*!

It was as though a tide had receded, revealing jagged rocks beneath a calm blue sea.

It was bad enough that he hadn't known until now exactly who Edmund Seymour was in relation to Prudence. But for her to suggest that Seymour now be allowed to give his 'opinion'— It was intolerable.

He gritted his teeth and then, turning to his grandfather, smiled gently. 'Papi, I'm going to sort this out. I want you to take the rest of the day off.'

He held his hand out towards his grandfather.

'You can go and put your feet up and read one of those interminable Russian novels you like so much.'

Waving away Janos's words of protest, he chivvied his grandfather out of the room.

'No, Papi. I insist. Prudence and I can manage.'

At the door, Laszlo stopped and turned, and she felt her pulse slam against her skin as his eyes fixed coldly on her face.

'Oh, don't ring your uncle just yet. I've got an opinion of my own I'd like to share with you first. Wait here!'

A moment later, her face still scalded with

colour, Prudence sat staring nervously around the dining room. Looking down at her plate, she pushed it away. Could she have misunderstood the implication of his words? But she knew she hadn't, and she knew that something had happened to change the mood between them. She frowned. Only *nothing* had happened. Part of her job was to reassure the client, and that was what she'd done. Her mouth tightened into a grim line. It most certainly *wasn't* part of her job to try to second-guess Laszlo's moods.

Ten minutes later she bit her lip in indecision and then, abruptly pushing back her chair, she stood up. Typical Laszlo! Telling her to wait and then forgetting all about her. She shook her head irritably. Unlike him, she actually had work to do. But first she would ring Edmund. After all, what possible objection could he really have to her speaking to her uncle?

Laszlo caught up with her just as she reached the cottage. 'Where the hell do you think you're going? I told you to wait!'

His voice, dark with fury, swung her round mid-stride. She stared at him, struck by the cold, angry beauty of his face.

Forcing herself to stay calm, she shrugged and

said flatly, 'I did wait. But you didn't come back and I have notes to write up. So, if you don't mind—'

'Oh, but I *do*. We need to talk.'

She flinched at the biting tone of his voice but drew her head up to meet his gaze. 'I'm sorry you feel like that, but I'm busy now,' she said carefully. 'Maybe we can talk later.'

Turning, her heart pounding in her chest, she walked quickly up the path and opened the front door of the cottage. Before she could shut it, Laszlo had followed her into the living room.

'What are you doing?' She stared at him furiously. 'You can't just barge in here!'

'Don't you *ever* walk away from me.' His face was twisted with anger. 'I told you to *wait*!'

She lifted her chin, eyes blazing. His high-handed manner was setting her teeth on edge. 'I did,' she shot back at him. 'But if you think I've got all day to sit around and wait for you—'

'My grandfather was upset. I was trying to make him feel better. But maybe you don't care about that.' His eyes were hardening like lava cooling.

'That's not true, Laszlo. I *do* care about your grandfather,' she said shakily. 'And I want to help. That's why I'm going to speak to my uncle.'

She stared at him in helpless silence as he shook his head.

'No, you're not.'

His voice scraped over her skin, hostility palpable in every syllable.

'Not if you want to keep this job!'

Prudence took a step backwards, the unfairness as much as the autocratic tone of his command leaving her feeling almost winded. She felt dizzy. He'd gone completely mad. That was the only explanation.

'What *is* your problem? You're not making any sense. If Edmund hadn't been ill he'd have been here instead of me. And you were fine with that. Only now you're telling me I can't even *ring* him?'

Incandescent with anger, Laszlo stared at her. She was right. His behaviour was irrational. Except that it wasn't. Only he couldn't explain that to her. Not while he was still reeling from this revelation that Edmund Seymour was the man who had ruined his life.

His chest felt tight and he took a calming breath. Finally, he said flatly, 'We made a deal. I told you that if you couldn't work for me then you should leave.'

'Any deal we made *didn't* include pussyfooting

around you when you're having some sort of temper tantrum!' She glared at him. 'This has nothing to do with our deal and you know it. You're just angry because I wasn't where you wanted me to be. Well, now you know what it feels like!'

There was a moment's savage silence and then she took a breath. What were they doing? Tearing each other apart over a phone call?

Feeling suddenly calmer, she shook her head and said slowly, 'I didn't just leave to make you angry. I really did—really *do*—have a lot of work to do.'

She bit her lip. Had they naively expected that the anger and resentment from their past would magically dissipate just because they'd started sleeping together again? If so, they'd been grievously mistaken. The fragile peace they'd shared for more than a week was over, and sadly she realised that it had been as illusory as every other aspect of their relationship.

'But my advice would still be to contact Edmund.'

His eyes narrowed. 'I see. I suppose you think you know better than I do what's best for my grandfather?'

Biting her lip, she nodded. 'In this instance—yes. He's worried about the cataloguing and Ed-

mund can help him,' she said simply. 'Sometimes
you just need a different point of view to solve the
problem.'

Catching sight of the ineffably contemptuous
sneer in his eyes, she felt a ripple of anger snake
over her skin.

She took a deep breath. 'You know, the trouble
with you, Laszlo, is you're just so certain you're
right you just can't imagine that there might be
another point of view.'

'Not true.' His voice was dangerously soft. 'I
know everything there is to know about other
points of view. Particularly your uncle's.'

There. He'd said it. It was as though he'd taken
off a particularly scratchy sweater. She stared at
him, her eyes blinking in time with her scattering
thoughts. 'What do you mean? You've never even
spoken to my uncle. He spoke to your grandfather
and Jakob.'

He smiled slowly and she felt the breath squeeze
out of her lungs.

'Not about the cataloguing…' he said softly.

'I don't understand,' she said faintly.

'Then let me explain.'

His voice seemed to slice her bones away from
her flesh and she felt her legs starting to sway.

'Seven years ago I went to your home.'

Her head jerked up and, despite the pain in his own heart, he felt a sharp sting of satisfaction at the shock in her eyes.

He looked at her steadily. 'I went to talk to you.'

Prudence's heart seemed to stop. 'I don't believe you,' she said weakly.

'That doesn't stop it being true.'

His voice trapped her, pulled her in. 'You're lying,' she whispered.

But she knew that he wasn't, and her face felt hot, and she suddenly couldn't breathe. Looking up, she saw the anger and the pride in his eyes. She took a step backwards.

Watching her back away, Laszlo felt a ripple of rage—even now she was trying to evade what she'd done.

'Only you were out. Shopping...' He spat the word out with derisive emphasis. *'Shopping!'* There was a tense, choking silence and he shook his head. 'How do you think that made me feel? To find out that while I was sitting in some stinking police station my wife was out shopping.' He laughed without humour. 'Sorry. My mistake. You didn't actually think we were married, did you?'

She clenched her fists. She had resolved never to

mention his arrest. But now his sneering contempt unleashed the pent-up fear and pain.

'What should I have been doing? We were over. Your criminal activities were no concern of mine.'

'They took me in for questioning. And then they released me without charge,' he said slowly, his face tight with hostility. 'Only you didn't know because you were out *shopping*.'

She shook her head, trying to stay focused. He didn't have the upper hand here—didn't have it full stop! All he'd done was lie and deceive her.

She glowered at him. 'We were over—'

'We were *not* over. We'd had a row. Do you really think I'd just let you throw away our marriage like that?' he said savagely. The air was quivering between them.

Prudence shook her head. 'I asked you how much effort you'd give to make our relationship work.' Her voice broke. 'Do you know what your answer was? You said that *any* effort was too much!'

'I was just angry with you! I'd just walked in the door. I was tired. I wanted a shower.'

Eyes blazing, she stepped towards him. 'And that meant you could give up on our relationship?'

'No. But as you keep on reminding me, I had to go to the police station!' His mouth twisted. 'I couldn't leave. You, on the other hand, were free. I came to find you as soon as I got out. You didn't come to see if I was all right.' He stopped and shot her a look of pure exasperation. 'I know that you didn't think our marriage was real. And, yes, we'd broken up. But didn't you feel bound to me in *any* way?'

The bitterness in his voice felt like a slap to her face.

There was a pulsing silence and then he shook his head. 'I could never work out what had changed. You seemed different that day. Not yourself.'

Prudence stared at him, trying to keep her expression steady. She could feel something like panic building up inside her.

He gave her a long, hard look. 'But then I met your uncle and it all kind of fell into place.' Smiling grimly, he nodded. 'You're right about his opinions, by the way. I didn't like what he had to say. In fact, I was quite upset by his point of view. But funnily enough I wasn't surprised by it.' He looked across at Prudence, his eyes glittering with sudden savage fury. 'But then, how could I be? I'd already heard it before—hadn't I?'

Prudence stared at him, frozen to the spot, struggling to swallow her shock. 'I don't understand...'

Her voice shrivelled as she felt the blistering anger of his gaze.

'Oh, I think you do.'

There was a moment's dead silence and then, in a voice that chilled her bones, he went on.

'When I'm struggling with something, I always find it helpful to have another point of view.'

She felt the blood drain from her face as she recognised her own words.

Watching her reaction, he clenched his jaw. 'It was quite eerie, actually. Hearing your words come out of his mouth. It was a faultless performance. You must have rehearsed a lot.'

'N-no…' Prudence stammered. 'No. It wasn't like that.' She shivered as the temperature in the room plummeted.

'It was *exactly* like that, Prudence. Or are you telling me he told you to stand by your man?'

Looking at her paper-white stricken face, he felt suddenly sick inside.

'No. I thought not.'

A muscle flickered in his jaw and he regarded her for a long, excruciating moment.

'You should have waited to hear what I had to say. But you didn't. You chose to listen to someone who'd never met me. Who despised the very idea of me.'

Laszlo leant forward, his face dark with fury.

'Do you know he called me a liar and a charlatan? Told me he knew all about my "sort".'

He gave a humourless laugh and Prudence felt her cheeks burn. She shook her head desperately.

'He didn't mean because you're a Romany,' she mumbled.

Laszlo smiled derisively. 'Please! Do you think I'm stupid?'

Miserably, Prudence shook her head. 'No. But I know he wasn't talking about that. He was just worried about me. About where it would all end. I think he thought I was turning into my mum.'

She looked away, fighting tears; fighting memories.

'You'd been gone for ten days, Laszlo. I didn't know what to think. I'd left so many messages, and then Edmund came home from work and found me crying.' She gave a small strangled laugh. 'I think it really scared him.' She drew a jagged breath. 'Especially because I hadn't really told him and Daisy much about us. Just that I was seeing someone I'd met at the fair.'

Prudence stared blankly around the sitting room.

'I *did* talk to Edmund, and he gave me advice. But he didn't change my mind,' she said slowly. 'When I came looking for you—after I'd spoken to him—I still wanted us to work. I would have done anything to be with you.' She paused and shivered, her lip trembling. 'But, like I told you before, you didn't even try and reassure me.'

Her voice petered out and Laszlo frowned. It was true. He *hadn't* tried to reassure her. And he saw now that the repercussions of her parents' bigamous marriage had affected not just Prudence but her aunt and uncle too. They had looked after her, brought her up. His breathing was suddenly harsh. How must it have felt for Edmund to see the girl he thought of as a daughter weeping hysterically over a man? A man who seemed in many ways to resemble her perfidious father?

Prudence took a breath and looked up at him sadly. 'Edmund told me what he thought I should do. But he also said that the decision must be mine.' She bit her lip and her eyes felt suddenly hot with tears. 'And it was. You didn't seem to care one way or another. That didn't seem to be a good basis for a relationship. So I ended it.'

Her stomach was contorting, as though her misery was actually alive inside her.

'Edmund didn't wrong you. All he and Daisy have ever done is try and protect me. You can think what you like. The truth is our relationship ended not because of other people or their opinions but because the sum of what we held back was greater than what we shared. We only really shared our bodies.'

Laszlo stared at her in silence. She had never looked more beautiful or vulnerable. But for once he couldn't lose himself in the soft beauty of her face. His skin was prickling with what he knew to be guilt. Guilt and regret. Having grown up in the shadow of her mother's disastrous love affair, she'd met him before she'd had a chance to realise that she wasn't her mother but her own person.

Now he understood just how lonely and frightened she must have felt when confronted by his baffling absences and moodiness. His head jerked up, his cheeks burning. He had told her he would never forgive her for what she'd done. Now he saw that it was he who needed forgiveness. He had been her lover and, in his mind at least, her husband. The one man who should have restored her faith in men and, more importantly, in herself.

And what had he done to reassure her?

Nothing.

No wonder she had sought comfort from the one man who had always been there for her and never let her down.

'You must love them very much,' he said finally.

He saw the flicker of emotion in her grey eyes.

'They're not perfect.' She smiled weakly. 'But they're my family, Laszlo, and I love them. I trust them too.'

'More than you trusted me?'

His question caught her off guard and she swallowed hard. She was so tired—more than tired… she was drained. Meeting his gaze, she saw from the tension around his eyes that her answer mattered to him. It would be easier to placate him; quicker to give him some glib answer that would end this row, so she could crawl off and lick her wounds. But she was done with lying to him. No matter what the consequences, she wanted to confront the past—the whole of the past. Not keep holding back or editing out the most painful parts.

Finally, she nodded.

The gold of his eyes began to flicker with outrage.

'What did you *want* me to say?' she said, annoyed by his reaction. 'Haven't you learned *anything* from the past? Our marriage might be over but I want—' She stopped. Her voice had turned husky with emotion but she didn't care. 'I need to be honest with you. And I'd like to think you want that too. So the answer is *yes*, Laszlo. I trusted them more than I trusted you. Or myself.'

His mouth set in a grim line, Laszlo stared at her for a long moment.

'I want to be honest with you as well,' he said quietly. 'You were right to have doubts about me. Right not to trust me.'

She stared at him dazedly. 'Wh—what do you mean?' she stammered. She felt almost physically sick at the expression of guilt and remorse on his face.

He watched her in silence, a muscle working in his jaw. 'I was holding back. Holding back the truth about my grandfather. And you sensed that and that's why you didn't trust me. Add that to all my comings and goings, and I'd say you had a very strong case for ending our relationship.'

He sucked in a breath.

'In fact, I'm surprised you stayed with me for so long.' His face tightened and then slowly, his hand shaking slightly, he reached out and stroked her cheek. 'I've not always been a kind person, *pireni*. Or a fair one.'

He let out the breath.

'When you broke up with me I blamed your uncle. And then I blamed you.' He gave a small, tight smile. 'And then I blamed both of you.' He sighed. 'But I can't blame anyone but myself for what happened. All I did was fuel your doubts and then get angry that you doubted me,' he said quietly. 'Too angry to look deeper.'

He opened his mouth to say something else and then stopped.

Prudence felt her spine stiffen, her hurt somehow tempered by the inevitability of the familiar way his face closed over. Had she really expected Laszlo to open up to her? Surely she knew him well enough to know that he would always have secrets to keep.

Frowning, Laszlo glanced away from the tears gleaming in her eyes. He didn't want to hurt her. She had been so open, so brave. But there was so much he couldn't explain.

'I'm sorry about everything,' he said slowly, 'but I'm glad we had this conversation.' There was a moment of uneven silence, and then his face creased and he added softly, 'And I'm glad you're here.'

He saw the pull of his words on her face and then

his chest tightened as he watched a tear trickle down her face.

'Don't cry!' Impulsively Laszlo reached out and brushed his fingers gently over her cheek. Their eyes locked and then he sighed again. 'We certainly didn't make it easy for ourselves, did we, *pireni*? I just assumed that our marriage would somehow magically work, and you were convinced it would fail!'

He tilted her face to his and cupped her chin in his hand.

'We didn't get everything wrong, though, did we? I mean, most couples would kill to have the sort of chemistry we share.'

She knew he didn't really mean his words to be taken seriously, but something about his remark depressed her. It was the truth, probably, she thought miserably. For Laszlo, any discussion about their relationship would always lead back to that one thing.

Glancing down at her, Laszlo frowned again. He knew he'd hurt her, and he wanted more than anything to pull her into his arms, but much as he desired her he suddenly didn't want to use sex to blot out emotion.

'Look, don't worry about the cataloguing.' He

paused and took a breath. 'I'm going to ring your uncle later and talk it all through with him. You don't think he'll recognise my voice, do you?'

Prudence hesitated a moment, her grey eyes searching his face. She knew he was trying to make amends and it was novel at least to have Laszlo be the one to make a peace offering. Shaking her head, she gave him a weak smile. He grinned at her and his obvious relief that he had made her smile made her heart wobble.

'Good. I don't want him charging over here to rescue you.' He paused. 'You don't *want* to be rescued, do you?'

Prudence shivered. Of course she didn't—but it might have been better if she had. Her feelings were becoming more and more confused, and harder and harder to contain.

She shook her head. 'No. I don't want to be rescued.'

His face flushed and she felt her pulse start to quicken, for he looked heartbreakingly like his younger self.

'I promise I'll be on my best behaviour,' he said slowly. 'I won't say or do anything annoying.'

She laughed softly. 'Let's not tempt fate!'

Looking down at her, Laszlo smiled crookedly.

'How reassuringly superstitious of you,' he said softly. 'My sweet Romany wife.'

She gazed at him, hypnotised by the soft darkness of his eyes and the even softer darkness of his voice. And then her heart twisted inside, for Laszlo's words were not a promise for the future but a simple statement of fact.

Trying to ignore the tangle of emotions her thoughts provoked, she glanced at one of the clocks—surely sense demanded she should leave before she said something she'd regret?

'I should go and find your grandfather, but he usually has a nap about now.' She bit her lip. 'I don't know what to do...'

Laszlo frowned. 'Maybe I can help with that.'

Sliding his fingers through her hair, Laszlo pulled her towards him, his expression thoughtful.

'Let's see...' Turning her hand over, he stroked the centre of her palm and then, lifting her hand, slowly ran his tongue along the lifeline until she squirmed against him. 'Hmm...' he murmured softly. 'Your skin's so smooth it's difficult to read the future. But...'

His gleaming golden gaze rested on her face, making her feel hot and tingly all over.

'I *can* see that there's a tall, dark, handsome man in your life.'

Prudence wriggled free and shook her head, trying not to laugh. 'Really? I wouldn't say Jakob is tall.'

He grinned at her. 'The man I'm talking about is definitely not a lawyer. He's just as smart, but he's witty and cool and sexy…'

He laughed softly as, heart pounding, she tugged her hand away. 'And bordering on the delusional?' she said quickly.

She wanted him so much. And when he held her close like this, his body so warm and hard against hers, everything inside her seemed to unravel and fly apart.

Hoping fervently that her feelings weren't showing on her face, she took a deep breath and lifted her chin. 'Or maybe you just need your eyes tested?'

He smiled—a long, curling smile that whipped at her senses.

'Quite probably. No doubt my eyes have been damaged by years of living in this gloomy castle.' He pressed his body against hers. 'Maybe I should keep you where I can see you,' he murmured possessively.

And then his hand tightened in her hair and, dropping a fierce kiss onto her lips, he pulled her into his arms.

CHAPTER EIGHT

FROM THE WINDOW of his bedroom Laszlo stared out at the cloudless blue sky and scowled. Rising early, he had gone for a walk before breakfast in the fields that surrounded the estate. Usually he enjoyed the silence and the crisp, early air—but not today. For once he had found it hard to take pleasure in the peace and beauty. Instead his thoughts had been dogged by scenes from last night. And now yesterday's conversation with Prudence was playing on repeat inside his head, so that rather than slip back into bed beside her, he'd returned to the castle.

His chest grew tight. Feeling distinctly uncomfortable, he closed the window. But there was no way he could shut out the unpalatable truth. He had treated her badly. And a weaker person—the person he'd so arrogantly assumed Prudence to be—would have been crushed.

Only she hadn't been crushed. And she hadn't given up either. In spite of her youth and inexperience, and in the face of his evident and repeated reluctance to talk about anything, she had still tried to make it work. His mouth tightened. And it was still the same story now. When fate had thrown them together he had used his power and position to punish her, but even then she hadn't walked away. She'd just climbed over the wall and refused to leave.

He suddenly grinned. He loved it that she was so bloody-minded. And beautiful. And brave. She was everything he'd wanted in a wife. And then his smile faded. Why was he using words like *wife* and *love*? He didn't *love* Prudence, and soon she wouldn't even be his wife. In fact, soon she wouldn't even be in the country. With a growl of frustration he clenched his hands. Everything seemed to have backfired. Letting Prudence back into his life and into his bed seemed to be having quite the opposite effect to the one he'd imagined.

For a start, sleeping with Prudence didn't actually seem to be killing his desire for her. If anything he wanted her more. In fact, he couldn't imagine a time when he *wouldn't* roll over in bed to find her lying next to him.

Worse, the anger he had felt when he'd found her in his study seemed to have faded to be replaced by a sort of nervous anticipation. He gritted his teeth. If he hadn't known better, he might have said that he had some sort of *feelings* for her.

A muscle flickered along his jaw. Only of course that would be ridiculous. His 'feelings' were just a trick of the senses. As Prudence had so rightly pointed out yesterday, the only time they ever felt comfortable being open and honest with one another was during sex, and no doubt his emotions were just the after-effects of intimacy. Add to that his guilt at having treated her so shabbily and it was no wonder he was feeling confused.

He let out a breath, pleased to have found a rational explanation for his discomfort. Glancing out of the window, he could just see the roof of the *vardo* and, whistling softly, he turned towards the door.

Sifting through the papers in his lap, Janos gave a small cry of triumph and beamed at Prudence.

'I've found it. *Finally.* That *is* a relief!' Glancing up, he looked at the grandfather clock in the corner of the sitting room and frowned. 'I can't imagine where Laszlo is.' He shook his head. 'Sometimes I think he's less house-trained than Besnik. At least Besnik remembers mealtimes.'

Closing her laptop, a blush creeping over her

cheeks, Prudence said shyly, 'Actually, he told me he's going to be a little delayed.'

Her blush deepened. She was still reeling from the unfamiliar experience of Laszlo earnestly *telling* her that he was going to be late.

Studiously avoiding Janos's eyes, she added, 'I think there was some problem over at the top field.'

Janos gave her a searching look. 'I see.' There was a pause, while Prudence gazed in concentration at the lid of her laptop, and then he said slowly, 'I think I might need to speak to your uncle later.'

Prudence looked up at him. 'Wh—why?' she stammered. 'Is there a problem?'

Janos shook his head, a small smile tugging at the corners of his mouth. 'Don't look so worried, my dear. I'm just wondering whether I can persuade him to let you stay for ever! First you manage to single-handedly organise forty years of paperwork concerning my collection, and now— far more impressively—you've trained my grandson to apprise you of his movements.'

Prudence drank a mouthful of coffee, finding it suddenly difficult to swallow. 'I don't think that's all down to me,' she said, blushing again.

Janos laughed. 'It's certainly not down to *me*! But don't worry. You won't have to stay in this draughty old castle for ever. I know you must be missing your family.'

She smiled. 'I did miss them at first. But you've made me feel so welcome. And I love the castle,' she said simply. 'It's such a perfect setting for all your beautiful things.' Biting her lip, she paused. 'Actually, it really reminds me of one of my favourite places—the Soane's Museum in London. Sir John Soane used to live there, with all these incredible works of art and sculptures and clocks— just like you do there. It's an amazing place.'

She shook her head slowly.

'Edmund says I treat it like church: I always go there if I have something to celebrate or if I feel sad—' She broke off in astonishment as the clocks throughout the castle began to strike the hour. 'Is that the time? Perhaps I'd better just run down and tell Rosa that Laszlo is—'

'Laszlo is what?'

Dressed casually in jeans and a faded grey sweatshirt, Laszlo strolled into the room, Besnik following at his heels. Reaching his grandfather's armchair, he bent down and kissed Janos gently on the head, then turned to Prudence, his gleaming gaze making her stomach flip over.

They shared a brief burning silence and then he

said, almost conversationally, 'That I'm starving? Or that I'm on time? Hard to say which would give her greater pleasure!'

Dropping onto a sofa, he sat back and his eyes drifted over her lips. Her breath stuck in her throat.

'How are you today, Prudence? Are *you* hungry too?'

His voice was teasing and warm, and she felt a corresponding heat across her skin. She glanced nervously over to Janos, for she was always worried that he would sense the tension between her and Laszlo. But she saw with relief that he had returned to sifting through his paperwork. She still disliked having to lie to him, but it was not for much longer. And then she would be back in England and she would have to lie only to herself.

She felt a jolt of misery. *Don't go there,* she told herself, sitting up straighter. *This was only ever going to be temporary. Nothing has changed.*

She took a deep breath. Only it had. She hadn't meant it to change, but it had. Like a tsunami warning, a cool voice inside her head kept urging her to get away from the strike zone. But she couldn't. Her only option was to stay detached. It was only sex, after all.

She shivered. But what was going on inside her

heart had nothing to do with sex. Her lower lip quivered as miserably she realised that Laszlo had been right all along. A piece of paper meant nothing. For in her heart she would always be married to Laszlo.

Shifting in her seat, she tried to steady her nerves. *It's all in your imagination,* she told herself angrily. But it wasn't. She loved him, and all she really wanted to do was forget everything that had happened between them and start again.

Looking up, her eyes collided with the stinging intensity of his gaze and she felt a spasm of pain— a pain that she knew no amount of distance in time or place would ever lessen. She might be in love with him, but he had simply and expediently reduced their relationship to the physical.

Heart pounding, fighting her misery, she looked away and said hastily, 'I'll just go and tell Rosa you're here.'

'Not necessary,' Laszlo said softly. 'I told her on my way up. Oh, and Jakob rang to say he'd be over this evening.'

He sat back, letting his long legs sprawl negligently in front of him, but despite his relaxed pose Prudence could almost see the restless energy coming off him in waves.

For a moment the room was silent, and then Janos looked across at his grandson thoughtfully. 'Incredible. You're on time *and* you remembered to give me a message!'

Laszlo shrugged. His face was neutral, but his feet were tapping out a rhythm on the carpet. 'Just keeping you on your toes, Papi.'

Janos studied his grandson benignly. 'There's nothing wrong with my toes. You, on the other hand, are about to wear a hole in one of my favourite rugs. Did Jakob say what time he'd be over?'

Frowning, Laszlo pretended to think. 'He did. Now, what did he say…? Oh, yes. About eight.' He grinned at his grandfather. 'Oh, ye of little faith!'

Shaking his head, Janos laughed. 'I'm impressed, but still a little shocked.'

'I don't see what the fuss is all about,' Laszlo grumbled. He turned to Prudence, a curve of amusement tugging at the corner of his mouth. 'What do *you* think, Prudence? Can't a leopard change his spots?'

Conscious of Janos's presence, she bit her tongue—but the desire to tease overwhelmed her. 'I'm not sure. Is that how you see yourself? As a leopard?'

She paused, mesmerised by the hunger burning

in his golden eyes and the rough shadow of dark stubble grazing his jaw.

'You're more like a wolf really,' she murmured, her blood slowing in her veins at the intensity of his gaze. 'A tamed wolf that'll come inside the house but only if the door is left open.'

Their eyes locked and she felt a shiver of quicksilver run down her spine. Suddenly her heart was pounding, and the only sound was the rain falling on the window and the strained intake of their breath.

And then Janos cleared his throat. 'I believe the word you're looking for is *liminal*,' he said mildly. 'It means to occupy a space on both sides of a boundary—or in this case threshold.'

For a moment Prudence stared at him blankly, all thoughts, all words gone. And then, colour burning her cheeks, she straightened up abruptly and the spell was broken.

'Liminal…I must remember that,' she said weakly, finding speech at last.

Janos nodded. 'I believe architects often refer to hallways as "liminal" spaces.'

Prudence shifted in her chair, uncomfortably aware that she'd been too consumed with longing to hide her emotions. But if Janos was aware of her feelings he was hiding it well, for he merely smiled and returned to reading his papers.

Her heart was thumping painfully hard. Breathing out, she looked up and found Laszlo watching her almost hungrily through the thick dark lashes that fringed his eyes.

'If I'm a wolf, does that mean you're a lamb?' he said softly. Her heart lurched against her ribs.

He was exactly like a wolf: a predatory, single-minded wild animal. And she felt exactly like a lamb that had stumbled into his lair. Only perhaps because finally—privately—she had admitted her love for him it suddenly felt like the most important thing in the world to disagree.

Taking a deep breath, she summoned up a casual smile. 'Oh, I'd probably be something very prickly and shy—like a hedgehog.'

Laszlo grinned slowly. 'Hedgehogs aren't always prickly. When they relax and feel safe their quills lie flat.'

Their eyes met and she had to curl her fingers into the palms of her hands to stop herself from reaching out and pulling his mouth against hers. 'Then what happens? You eat them, I suppose?'

She blushed as he lifted an eyebrow.

'That would depend on the hedgehog.'

Janos shook his head. 'He's teasing you, my dear. He's never eaten a hedgehog in his life.'

Smiling weakly, Prudence sat up straighter, flattening herself against the back of the chair. Her skin felt hot and prickling, quite as if she were growing spines, and she had to ball her hands into fists to stop herself from rubbing her arms.

'What about you, Janos?' she said quickly, turning away as Laszlo mouthed the word *coward* at her. 'What animal are *you* like?'

Janos put down his papers and frowned. 'Judging by the state of my memory, I ought by rights to be a goldfish,' he said ruefully.

They all burst out laughing.

Grinning, Laszlo reached across and squeezed his grandfather's hand. 'You're such a fraud, Papi! Your memory's better than mine. And as for Prudence—' He shook his head. 'Hers is *too* good! I'd like her to forget the odd thing.'

He paused and, unable to resist the pull of his gaze, Prudence looked up helplessly.

He gave her a crooked smile and then his expression shifted, grew suddenly serious. 'Actually, there's quite a lot of things I'd like her to forget.' He hesitated, as though groping in his mind for a word or phrase, and then said quietly, 'Quite a lot I'd want to change too.'

She stared at him uncertainly, her stomach suddenly churning with nerves and confusion. His voice was strained—she might even have described it as anxious. But of course that must be her nerves playing with her imagination, for his face was neither.

Something passed through his eyes, and then abruptly he stood up and walked over to his grandfather.

'Papi! I've got some news! Something I want to share with you!'

Looking up, Janos chuckled and shook his head slowly. 'I *knew* there was something. I don't know about a wolf, but you've been like a cat on a hot tin roof all morning! Come on, then—out with it. What's your news?'

'Kajan is here!' Laszlo spoke softly but his eyes were bright.

Prudence smiled politely. She had no idea who Kajan was, but his arrival was obviously welcome, for both men were beaming at each other.

'He arrived last night, after you'd gone up to bed. I helped him set everything up in the top field. Everyone else should be arriving today.'

He hesitated and Prudence felt her scalp begin to prickle, for she could hear the pent-up excitement in his voice.

'Mihaly wants to christen Pavel this weekend. And they've asked *me* to be his godfather.' Then he grinned as Janos stood up shakily and pulled his grandson into his arms.

Watching them together, Prudence felt suddenly utterly out of place—as though she had gatecrashed a private party. Inside, her heart felt leaden. Lying in his arms that morning, her body aching and sated, their closeness had felt like the natural, unfeigned intimacy of any normal couple—it had been easy to pretend to herself that theirs was just an ordinary relationship.

But now, like a spectator watching from the sidelines, she felt a stab of despair. Who was she kidding? She had no right to stand up and congratulate her lover with a hug. Nor would she ever see his godfathering skills put into practice with their own children.

Forcing herself to push away that troubling thought, she smiled brightly and said, 'Congratulations. That's wonderful!'

Releasing his grandfather, Laszlo turned towards

her. She was about to repeat her congratulations when something on his face stopped her.

'Thanks.'

He stared at her with such bleakness that she felt cold on the inside.

And then his face twisted into a smile as his grandfather patted his arm and said shakily, 'I'm very, *very* proud of you. I'm sorry, my dear!' Janos glanced at Prudence. 'It's just that this is quite a moment for both of us.'

She smiled at Janos. 'Of course it is! And I'm very pleased for both of you.' Her gaze flickered towards Laszlo and she said carefully, 'What are your duties? Is it quite a hands-on role?'

His eyes fixed on her face and she saw a ripple of some nameless emotion stir the surface.

Then, glancing away, he shrugged and said stiffly, 'It can be.'

His voice was flat, with no trace of his earlier joy, and she could almost see him withdrawing from the conversation—withdrawing from *her*. She stared at him in misery and confusion.

'I'm sure Mihaly will want you to be involved,' she said slowly. 'He obviously thinks a lot of you.'

He shrugged. There was a short, tense silence and then, not looking at her, he said coolly, 'I'm his cousin. Relatives are always chosen to be god-parents.'

'I didn't know,' she said stiffly.

'Why should you?'

The coldness in his voice held a warning. It felt like a slap to the face and, biting her lip, she looked away. She felt suddenly foolish and tired—for how could she ever have imagined that they were close?

Oblivious to the tension in the room, Janos beamed. 'He's following a great tradition, Prudence. Both his father and his father's father had many godchildren between them, and I know Laszlo will be the same. He is much loved.' His face softened and he glanced at Prudence conspiratorially. 'And this will be good for him. Being shut up in this castle with only an old man for company has made him far too serious about life.'

Avoiding Laszlo's gaze, Prudence licked her lips. 'He *can* be a little intense,' she said carefully.

Janos snorted and Laszlo looked up and shook his head. 'I *am* still in the room, you know,' he said drily.

Prudence eyed him sideways. His mood seemed to have shifted again, and not for the first time she wondered what actually went on inside that handsome head of his. She watched in silence as he sighed in mock outrage.

'Some of us don't spend all day just looking at pretty pictures, Papi. So, now that my character is slain—laid bare and lifeless for all to see—can we move on? I've got a lot to organise.'

He was smiling again and Janos laughed.

'Is that right? I'll remind Rosa of that later!' Reaching into his jacket pocket, he pulled out a small leather-bound notebook and a fountain pen. 'We're all going to be very busy for the next few days. You too, my dear,' he said, smiling warmly at Prudence. 'Outsiders don't generally get to go to Romany gatherings, but you're our guest, so you'll be welcomed as one of the family.'

Prudence felt the blood drain from her face. She glanced anxiously across at Laszlo, to gauge his re-action to Janos's words, but he was leaning forward unconcernedly, scratching Besnik's ears. Perhaps he hadn't heard—for surely if he had he would be making some sort of objection? After all, he wouldn't actually *want* her mixing with his family. It had been nerve-racking enough meeting Mihaly.

Janos looked up and frowned. 'I imagine Kajan will be wanting a *bolimos* after the christening?' He turned towards Prudence. 'Kajan is the most senior member of the Cziffra family. Between the two of us, we brought Laszlo up.'

Feeling slightly sick, Prudence nodded weakly. If only Laszlo would pay attention!

She felt a swell of relief as he looked up distractedly and frowned. Thank goodness! Now he would intervene and tell Janos that she couldn't possibly come to some intimate family gathering.

But after a moment, he simply nodded and said, 'Yes. I was thinking we might hold it in the barn. We'll need that much room for the tables and the dancing.'

Janos glanced across to where Prudence sat, quietly frozen, looking at her hands. 'A *bolimos* is great fun. It's like a huge feast and party combined. And the whole *kumpania* turn out for one. Men, women, children… So you'll have a chance to meet everyone.'

Prudence forced herself to smile. 'That's really very kind of you, but I don't think I should intrude—'

Frowning, Janos glanced up at the clock. 'Nonsense. Laszlo—make Prudence see sense. I am going to find Rosa, and then we'll all have a glass of champagne to celebrate.'

Wordlessly, Prudence watched him leave, and

then, turning to Laszlo, she said breathlessly, 'Why didn't you say something? You know I can't come!'

He narrowed his eyes. 'Seriously? You're worried about *intruding*? Shall I remind you of how you got your job back?'

'Of course I'm not worried about intruding,' she said crossly. Why was he being so obtuse? 'If you won't say something then I'll have to speak to your grandfather...'

He frowned. 'It's just a christening and a party.'

She looked at him incredulously. 'But you don't know who's going to be there. What if someone recognises me?'

He shrugged. 'They won't. But even if they did, like I said, they wouldn't say anything.' He studied her for a moment with that mixture of bafflement and irritation she knew so well, and then, at last, he said softly, 'Besides, they won't remember you. There were always loads of *gadje* girls hanging round the site. I doubt they could tell any of you apart.'

Prudence shivered. She felt numb inside. How could a few randomly combined words cause so much pain? And how could he be so insensitive, so brutal when he'd been so loving just hours ago? But then, love had nothing to do with his earlier tenderness during sex. His kisses and caresses were simply designed to excite and arouse. Any impression of feeling was a mistake on her part.

'I see.'

Her response was automatic. She'd just needed to say something—anything to slow the suffocating, relentless misery rolling over her. And it worked, for anger was slowly supplanting the exhaustion.

'Let's hope that's true for both our sakes. And now I think I'll go and look at some pretty pictures!'

She stood up quickly, but he was quicker.

'I'm sorry!'

His voice was so taut, so savage that it took her a moment to understand that he was apologising.

'What?' she said dazedly. 'What did you say?'

She watched him shake his head, saw muscle tighten beneath his shirt and thought that she must have misheard him.

And then he said quietly, 'I'm sorry. I shouldn't have spoken to you like that. I didn't mean what I said.'

His words seemed to be scrabbling out of his mouth, and with shock she saw that there was fear and misery in his eyes.

'I'm sorry,' he muttered again. 'Don't go. Please.'

Prudence regarded him in silence. Even though he'd hurt her so badly, she felt an urge to reach out and comfort him. Stifling it, she lifted her chin. 'Why did you say it, then?'

He shook his head again. 'I don't know. To hurt you, I suppose.'

She stared at him. 'Why do you want to hurt me?' she said slowly. 'I thought we were past all that. You said you wanted me to forget and that you wanted to change—'

Laszlo grimaced.

'And I meant it,' he said shakily. 'But then, when I told my grandfather this morning about being a godfather, I just kept thinking about all the lies I've told him and how badly I treated you—' His face twisted. 'I just don't think I can stand up in front of all those people and make promises.'

Prudence swallowed. She felt helpless in the face of his uncertainty, for Laszlo had always been so sure, so secure in his beliefs.

'Why not?' She looked up at his face and then, taking a breath, reached out and took his hand. 'Why not?' she repeated.

He stared down at her hand almost in bewilderment, and for a moment Prudence thought he would push it away. But instead his fingers tightened on hers and she had to bite back tears.

'Surely you, of all people, don't need to ask me that?' he said quietly.

His eyes fixed on her face and she realised with astonishment that she did. She had actually forgotten what had happened between them. Her breath stilled. Forgotten and forgiven—for of course she loved him, and what purer form of love was there but forgiveness?

'Mihaly wouldn't have asked you to be a godparent if he didn't think you could do it.'

He looked away, his face creasing with frustration. 'I told you. Mihaly chose me because I'm family. And family comes first,' he muttered hoarsely.

Prudence's eyes blazed. 'And who knows that more than you? Janos told me how you stayed with him the whole time your grandmother was ill. And you're still here now, taking care of him.'

She paused, her words and the emotion behind them choking her.

'Look at *me*!' she commanded. 'You even let me stay to make him happy. Despite everything that had happened between us you let it go. For *him*.' She shook her head. 'You're strong and loyal and kind. And I think you'll be a wonderful godfather.'

There was a moment's charged silence and then Laszlo lifted her hands to his lips and kissed them tenderly. 'So. When did you become my number one fan, *pireni*?' he murmured unsteadily.

Lost in the golden softness of his gaze, she let out a long, shaking breath. 'I'm not saying there's not room for improvement...' she said slowly.

He smiled and she saw that his misery and confusion was fading and his confidence had returned too, and also a peace that hadn't been there before—as though something...some burden...had been lifted from his shoulders.

'Is that so?' he asked lightly. 'Perhaps you could give me a little bit of guidance. Point me in the right direction!'

He ran his hand lightly down her arm, his fingers brushing against her breast. She nodded, grateful that his words required no answer, for her mind was struggling to think of something other than the touch of his hands on her skin.

But even as she let him pull her closer her relief was tinged with confusion. Not so many days ago she had hated Laszlo. Now she was championing his cause, and with a joy almost like a jolt of pain she realised that for the first time ever he had needed her.

She felt his hand moving rhythmically over her back, lower and lower. But what did any of that matter really? She might love Laszlo, but for him this relationship was only ever going to be about great sex. Nothing would change that. But she could change how she reacted to that fact like when she'd been a child and she'd wanted a star for her birthday. Eventually she'd got over it and settled for a dolls' house. That was what you did when you wanted the impossible. You took what was offered instead. And if all Laszlo could offer was passion, then she wasn't going to dwell on the impossible.

'Why are you shivering? Are you cold?'

'No,' she said and swallowed.

Gently, his breathing not quite steady, he pulled her closer. She felt the warmth of his body against her and some of her confusion seemed to go away. And then his arms tightened and, leaning against him, she reached up and pulled his mouth onto hers, kissing him with fierce desperation.

Blindly, he pulled her closer, pressing her against him, deepening the kiss, tasting, teasing, tracing the shape of her lips. Prudence whimpered. Her skin was squirming with tension, drops of plea-sure spreading over her skin in rippling concentric circles. She could feel her body melting; feel his hardening, the swollen length of his arousal pressing against her pelvis.

His grip tightened in her hair and she felt him shudder—and then he groaned softly and pushed her away.

'Wh—what's the matter?' She took a step backwards, gripping his shirt to steady herself. 'Why have you stopped?'

Laszlo gave a strangled smile. 'I want to tear all your clothes off.' He glanced over his shoulder. 'But Rosa will be up here any minute. We need some place private.' He felt a flash of panic: he sounded like some gauche teenage boy.

'So take me somewhere private. Somewhere I can tear your clothes off,' she said slowly.

Groaning, he lowered his mouth and kissed her fiercely. And then from the hallway there was the sound of voices and laughter and he tore his lips away from hers. They stared at each other, panting, and then finally he held out his hand.

'Come with me!'

CHAPTER NINE

HAND IN HAND they ran, giggling like teenagers, past an open-mouthed Rosa, along corridors and up staircases, until finally he stopped and they stood panting in front of a door.

Heart thudding, feeling a knot of tension in her stomach, Prudence stared at him. 'Where are we?'

He was silent, and then abruptly he leant forward and, tipping her head back, kissed her hard—kissed her until she couldn't think or speak or breathe.

He lifted his head and stared into her eyes. 'Somewhere private,' he said softly. 'My bedroom.'

With infinite tenderness he ran his fingers over her trembling cheek, his eyes fixing on hers.

'You don't need to worry about being disturbed. No one comes up here but me.'

She stared at him for a long moment, her chest tightening, for she knew he was trying to let her know that this was important to him. Wordlessly, she nodded, her breath sharpening at the blazing, possessive intensity of his gaze, and then his head dropped and his mouth captured hers, parting her lips and kissing her passionately.

Suddenly he was pushing her backwards, through the door and across the room to the bed. Her hands slid over his back and through his hair, and then she cried out hoarsely as his lips slid down her neck and over her throat and collarbone, grazing her nipples through the thin fabric of her blouse.

One hand was on her hip, the pressure making her squirm against him. Her eyes closed as his warm breath caressed her throat. She felt cool air on her thighs as slowly his fingers pushed up the hem of her skirt. And then his hands moved higher and gently he pulled the silken strip of her panties from her.

He lifted his head and gazed down at her, breathing unsteadily, his eyes dark with passion. 'You are so beautiful,' he murmured. 'And I want you so much.'

Dry-mouthed, she watched him slide down the bed. 'What are you—?'

But her words died on her lips as he dipped his head and lowered his mouth to the small triangle of damp curls at the top of her pelvis. She gasped, squirming beneath his touch, almost frightened at how badly she wanted him to keep touching her. Her pulse was pounding; her skin felt hot, burning with a fierce white heat. Inside she was tightening, her body tugging her towards the darkness.

Curving her back, she balled her hands into fists, curling and uncurling as she felt his warm, flickering tongue probe and caress. Suddenly her head was spinning. She clutched him closer and a fluttering, dancing pleasure shimmered over her skin, growing faster and stronger, quickening in time to her pulse, until finally her body tensed and she arched her pelvis against his mouth, burying her hands in his hair.

She lay spent and shaken, and then he slid back up the bed. She shuddered helplessly as his tongue found the soft swell of her breast. Moaning softly, she pulled frantically at the buttons of his fly, her breath stuttering in her throat as she felt the hard, straining male flesh as she eased his jeans down.

At the touch of her hand he groaned and, reaching out blindly, she pulled him inside her. His hips lifted to meet hers and he thrust deep inside, then deeper still, his mouth capturing hers. She gripped his arms, her body throbbing in response, moving and shifting frantically against him. His hands tightened convulsively in her hair and his mouth sought hers. Her muscles clenched and, digging her nails into his back, she cried out loud as her entire body jerked against his. And then she heard his own cry as he tensed, arched and drove himself inside her.

Later, their bodies aching and sated, they lay entwined on his bed.

'I meant to ask you something, earlier.'

His deep voice broke into her thoughts and she tipped her head up to gaze at him. 'What is it?'

He smiled, his eyes lighting up as they moved over her face and body. 'I wanted to ask you why you came back. The second time, I mean.'

She frowned. 'I told you. To get my job back.'

He nodded. 'But there are other jobs. Surely no job was worth having to put up with me?' Raising his eyebrow, he studied her face, watching the slow flush of colour spread over her skin.

'I didn't want to let my uncle down.'

She looked up at him, her eyes wide with misery and confusion, and he felt a sudden fiercely protective rush towards her.

'You didn't. But if you'd told him who I was he wouldn't have wanted you to stay—?'

She shook her head. 'I couldn't tell him. He needs the money,' she said flatly. 'Edmund's stupidly generous with everyone and he's got in a muddle. Anyway… Your fee will make everything okay. That's why I had to come back.'

His eyes were warm and clear, like single malt whisky. 'I see. So you put up with me to make your uncle happy? Despite everything that happened between us, you let it go? For *him*.' He shook his head. 'I think that makes *you* pretty strong and loyal and kind too.'

Recognising her words, Prudence blushed.

Laszlo frowned. 'You know, we might be more like one another than we care to admit. I think if we'd concentrated on how similar we are, rather than focusing on our differences, we could've made it work.'

Smiling, she slid her hand low over his belly, watching his eyes close with relief—for her sadness was almost too much to bear beneath his gaze. They had wasted what they might have had and yet she knew that one word from him and she would have given their marriage another chance.

But Laszlo was only talking about the past. Words like *if* and *could've* held no promise of a future they might share. Her throat was suddenly thick and tight with tears, and then she felt his hand curl underneath her and, closing her eyes too, she let the fire building inside her consume her misery…

Later, running her hand lightly over his hair-roughened skin, still intoxicated with happiness at how much he'd wanted her, Prudence buried her face against the hard muscles of his chest.

'You smell gorgeous,' she murmured. Tilting her head back, she met his eyes. 'Like woodsmoke and lemons and salt, all mixed up.'

Laszlo held her gaze and then gently kissed her on the lips. 'How is that "gorgeous"? It sounds like kippers to me.'

Laughing softly, she cuffed him playfully around the head and then, giving a shiver of pleasure, snuggled against him. She felt ridiculously happy and safe. Outside the sun was shining weakly, and she could hear birds singing, but it was what was inside his room that mattered. Just her and Laszlo: perfect and complete. Here they could laugh and kiss and touch, and the uncontrollable, intrusive demands of the outside world would just pass them by.

Drowsily, she pressed herself against him.

She didn't remember falling asleep. With a sigh, she rolled over onto her side and, opening her eyes, found Laszlo, fully clothed, sitting on the edge of the bed watching her.

'You got up…' she murmured sleepily, stretching out under the sheets.

Smiling, he lowered his head and kissed her—a teasing caress of a kiss that made her feel hot and tense, made her want him all over again.

'Why don't you come back to bed?' She sat up, the sheet slipping down over her body, exposing her breasts, and watched his gaze darken and grow blunt and focused. She shivered with anticipation.

'I want to….'

He ran his fingers over the smooth, flat curve of her abdomen and she swallowed as a prickling heat spread over her. 'But…?'

He glanced at her regretfully and then shook his head. 'But I can't. I just went downstairs to grab some food and my uncle collared me—now I've got to paint the barn with my cousins.' Glancing from her breasts to her reproachful face, he groaned. 'Don't look at me like that! If I don't go down they'll come looking for me—'

Glancing towards the door, he frowned and picked up one of his sweaters from a nearby chair.

'In fact, I wouldn't put it past them to come barging up here anyway. Let's get you decent.'

Prudence frowned. 'I can just get dressed and go.'

She watched his face shift, grow hesitant, and then he shook his head slowly.

'No. I don't want you to leave.'

Her heart gave a tiny leap. His desire for her to stay was obviously nothing more than that: desire. But he clearly didn't want her to leave, which was something.

Feeling suddenly wicked, she leant against the pillow and let the sheet slip even lower. 'Won't they knock?' she asked mischievously.

He glared at her. 'No. They won't. Now—arms up,' he said firmly.

Pretending not to notice how aroused he was, Prudence raised her arms with exaggerated slowness. Swearing softly under his breath, he slid the jumper down and over her head.

'That's better,' he said, breathing out. Grimacing, he shook his head. 'You are going to pay for that later, *pireni*.' His body stiffened painfully as he heard her breath quicken. 'Damn it!' Shaking his head, he laughed softly. 'You have got to stop taking advantage of me. Or at least feed me first. If we hadn't missed lunch I'd never have gone downstairs and Kajan wouldn't have collared me.'

Food. Lunch.

Prudence stared at Laszlo, frozen in horror as

her stomach suddenly gave a loud grumble of complaint.

'Oh, no! W-we missed lunch!' she stammered, staring at him in dismay.

Laszlo shrugged.

'It's cool. I saw Papi and told him you were lying down.'

She gaped at him. 'Up *here*?' she squeaked. 'You told him I was in your bedroom?' Her cheeks felt suddenly hot, and she felt panic rising like a storm inside her.

Laszlo frowned. 'I'm thirty, Prudence, not fourteen. I don't have to ask permission to take people up to my room. Anyway, don't look so worried.' He leant forward and kissed her. 'He was fine about it. He told me to let you sleep. Said that you'd been working far too hard. And Rosa was just worried that you'd starve. Which reminds me…'

Pausing, he stood up and walked across to the chest of drawers, picked up a plate covered with a napkin.

'I made us a picnic.' He grinned, his eyes gleaming. 'Oh, and there are cherries. Unless you want to wait till I get back for dessert?'

She rolled her eyes at him and laughing softly, he sat down on the bed beside her.

While they ate he told her stories about the castle and explained some of Hungary's complicated history. Then, when they'd finished, they fed each other cherries until there was nothing but stones and stalks left. Finally Prudence looked up and kissed him softly on the lips.

'Thank you. That was delicious. Some quite surprising taste combinations. I like that.'

She was teasing him and he grinned.

'I know you like to mix your flavours up.'

She shivered as his warm hand touched the bare skin of her leg.

'But what if I could only give you bread and cheese? Would you be happy with that?' he asked slowly.

'Yes,' she said softly. 'If you were there I'd eat old shoe leather.'

His eyes were dark and unreadable and then, glancing away, he looked round the room speculatively. 'Maybe you should just stay here in the tower? You could be my very own Lady of Shalott.'

She looked at him levelly, trying to ignore the steady, soft touch of his hands. Trying to stop herself from reading too much into his remark. She smiled. 'Doesn't she die alone and heartbroken?'

Laszlo frowned.

'Yes, she does. I'd forgotten that part. I wasn't really thinking about the poem. I just remember the painting by Waterhouse.' He smiled at her mockingly. 'Okay. What about Rapunzel? She saves her prince and they live happily ever after.'

Not trusting herself to speak, Prudence glanced away. *Could* she save Laszlo? Would he ever let her get close to him? She felt a flicker of hope. Maybe they could live happily ever after—maybe that was why fate had thrown them back together.

Her breathing slowed. Wrapped up in his bed sheets, it was easy to forget that none of this was real, for his words were so seductive. But her relationship with Laszlo would end soon, and there would be no happy-ever-after. And his words were designed to captivate and ensure that he got what he wanted. She sighed. What she had wanted too, at the beginning. Only now she wanted more.

And then, remembering how he'd held back from her just yesterday, she felt her stomach tighten. There was no point in hoping for any kind of reconciliation. What kind of marriage could they really have without trust and openness on both sides? Not that Laszlo had any interest in rekindling their relationship anyway. To him, this was and had only ever been a finite fling. Any seduction on his part was simply a means to an end. She needed to remember that when his poetic words started making her believe in fairy tales.

Composing herself, she smiled. 'I'm not sure. I don't remember Rapunzel throwing suitcases at her prince,' she said teasingly.

He gave her a crooked smile. 'That's because her pointy hat got in the way.'

She giggled as he reached over and pulled her closer.

'Not that you've thrown anything at me for days. Except the odd insult!' His eyes moved across her face slowly. 'I meant what I said. About you staying. I mean, why does all of this have to end?'

His arm tightened around her waist.

'I admit when you arrived it was difficult. We had a lot of things to sort out. But that's done now.'

His face was tense with concentration; she knew he was choosing his words carefully.

'We could just carry on doing what we're doing, couldn't we? We both want it. And I want you more than I've wanted any other woman.'

She felt a twitch of longing between her thighs, but it was tempered with sadness. It was flattering to be so desired, only she wanted so much more.

But the thought of leaving him was so dreadful to contemplate that there was really no point pretending that she would refuse a relationship on whatever terms he offered.

'Just you and me? Just the two of us?' she said lightly.

He nodded, but his expression was suddenly serious. 'Just the two of us,' he echoed. 'That could work.'

Silence fell and then abruptly, Laszlo stood up.

'I'd better go. But you'll stay, won't you?'

She nodded slowly and watched him leave and then, sighing, she fell back onto the pillows.

She hadn't meant to fall asleep again. But somehow she had. It was the second time she had woken up in Laszlo's bed. Only this time she was alone in his room, and she felt his absence like an ache inside. Hugging his jumper against her body, she drew some comfort from his scent, and then rolling over, she gazed around the room.

It was a beautiful room, with high ceilings and deep, wide-set windows. Unlike all the other rooms she'd seen at the castle, there were no paintings or mirrors on the pale grey walls and it was sparsely furnished. Just an armchair, the curved wooden bed she was lying on and a chest of drawers.

And then she noticed the photograph.

For a moment, she stared at it blankly, wondering why she hadn't noticed it before, for it was the only ornament in the room. Then, pushing back the sheets, she walked across the carpet and, feeling slightly guilty, reached out and touched the framed black and white photograph.

Her mind was humming. Thoughts and feelings were buzzing through her head. And then she breathed in sharply. The two people in the photograph were Laszlo's parents. She was sure of it. The family resemblance was there in every line and curve of their faces. They were so beautiful, so young. But what drew her eye was not their youth or beauty—it was the intensity of their focus. They literally seemed to have eyes for no one but each other.

Prudence swallowed. She had never seen a photo of her own parents together. In fact, the only picture she had of her father was from a newspaper. Someone—probably Aunt Daisy—had cut out the report of a trial involving her father. She'd found it, yellowing and fading, hidden inside a book.

She was gazing so intently at the photograph that she didn't hear Laszlo come in.

'Pick it up, if you want.'

Jumping slightly at the sound of his voice, she turned round, a faint blush colouring her cheeks. 'You always seem to catch me snooping,' she grumbled.

Watching her worry the soft flesh of her lower lip, he felt a sudden twitch of desire. Even wearing his tatty jumper, with her hair tousled from sleep and her pink mouth bruised from his kisses, she looked sexier than hell.

He gave her a faint smile. 'Snooping...breaking and entering? Prudence, I have a feeling you're not in Surrey any more!'

There was a short, tense silence and then he reached out for her as she stepped towards him and they kissed fiercely.

Lifting his head, he dragged his mouth away from hers. 'I missed you.' He felt her arms tighten around him.

'I missed you too,' she murmured, burying her face against his chest.

Finally she gestured towards the photograph and frowned.

'Sorry...' She hesitated. 'They're your parents, aren't they?'

He nodded slowly, his golden eyes studying her warily. 'Yes.'

'Is that before or after they were married?'

'After,' he said shortly.

She wanted to ask more, but the brusqueness of his tone seemed to discourage any more talk in that direction, so instead she glanced around the room and said lightly, 'It's not how I expected it to look. Your room, I mean.'

'What were you expecting? Shawls and knick-knacks and bargeware?' Seeing from her guilty expression that she had, he grimaced and shook his head. 'I've had my fill of castles and roses—excuse the pun. But why do you care what my room looks like?' And then he frowned. 'Oh, I get it. You think it somehow reflects *my soul.*'

His earlier tension seemed to have shifted and his eyes were laughing down at her.

She blushed. 'I did an Art History degree, remember? I can find tragedy and torment in two squares of maroon and red.'

Grinning, he took her hand and held it against his lips. 'So what do you think my room says about me?'

She lifted her head. 'I think it says you ran out of picture hooks. Either that or you're a philistine.'

She yelped as he made a grab for her.

'Just because I don't want a bunch of Old Masters cluttering up my walls, it doesn't make me a philistine.'

He spoke flippantly, but there was an edge to his voice and she turned to face him.

'I was joking. Truly. I know you're not a philistine,' she said slowly.

She watched his face grow taut.

'Because of my grandfather?' He shrugged. 'That's rather a simplistic point of view. I would have thought you'd be the first person to understand that blood can be no thicker than water.'

He looked away, and her cheeks burning, Prudence stared at his profile helplessly. There was something pushing to get out from behind his anger. Something that he'd wanted and failed to tell her yesterday and she needed to find some way—some words—to reach him.

Holding her breath, she followed his gaze. He was looking at the photograph of his parents.

'What were they like?'

He was silent so long she thought he wasn't going

to reply, and then his shoulders rose and fell and he said quietly, 'They were perfect.'

Her heart was suddenly pounding. It was an odd word to use, but it was the way he said it—so wearily, so unhappily—that made her feel as though she were breaking in two.

Her eyes fixed on the photograph.

'You look a lot like your mother,' she said carefully. 'But your eyes are just like your father's.'

Laszlo watched her glance anxiously from the photo back to him. 'At least I inherited *something* from them.'

He hadn't meant his remark to sound so sharp, and his neck tensed as she turned to look at him.

'What does that mean?'

Instead of answering he gave a casual shrug and leant forward, intending to kiss her. Kiss away his pain and confusion.

But, stepping backwards, she stared at him confusedly. 'I want to help—'

'I don't want your help!'

He spoke quickly—too quickly—and she lifted her head, her eyes suddenly darker than steel, her voice glacier-cold. 'But you *do* want to have sex with me?'

As he met her gaze, he felt relief, for her anger

was so much easier to respond to than her concern. 'I don't see a connection.'

'I want you to stop pushing me away.'

'I don't push you away. I can barely keep my hands off you.'

'I'm not talking about that. That's just sex.'

She looked away. There was a pulsing silence. A muscle flickered in his jaw and he groped for something to take the pain from her eyes. And from his heart.

'I'm sorry. I don't want to.' His face was suddenly stiff with tension. 'I'm not trying to push you away—' Prudence stared at him anxiously. She could almost feel the weight of misery in his heart.

'But you are pushing *something* away. Or someone…?'

It was conjecture—nothing more than a feeling—but his face tightened.

'Is it your mum and dad?'

He looked almost dazed, and then his eyes seemed to scramble away from hers. There was a silence, and then he said quietly, 'I let them down. And not just them. My grandparents too.'

'I don't understand…' she said slowly. And then suddenly—incredibly—she did. 'Are you talking about our marriage?'

Even as he nodded, she was shaking her head.

'No. Laszlo. That doesn't make sense. None of them knew about our marriage. So how could you have let them down?'

His face quivered. 'You're right. You *don't* understand.' He frowned. 'Even now people in my family talk about my parents. They were so perfect together. And they made everything look so effortless. Marriage. Love. Life.'

He grimaced. Even the difference in their backgrounds had been no obstacle to their happiness; instead their passionate belief in each other had simply blurred the lines between the Romany and non-Romany world.

'And you wanted to be like them.' It was a statement not a question.

After a brief hesitation he let out a breath and nodded. 'I wanted what they had. That passion—that rightness.' He gave a twisted smile. 'I think, actually, it'd be more accurate to say that, as their son, I *expected* it. As my right. And I thought I had it.'

'Why?' she whispered.

And she was suddenly more grateful than she'd ever been that it was his turn to speak, for she couldn't have opened her mouth again without crying.

'I met you.' He smiled again, but this time his smile seemed to illuminate his whole face. 'And I was desperate—no, *determined* not to lose you. We married and everything was perfect. At first.'

She stared at him, feeling a spasm of nausea. 'And then I ruined it?'

Abruptly he grabbed her arms and shook her, his face tightening with anger. 'No. You *didn't* ruin it. You were just young and nervous and inexperienced.'

She struggled against him, words tumbling haphazardly from her lips. 'You were young too.'

'Spoilt and arrogant is what I was! I was used to getting what I wanted,' he said harshly. 'And what I wanted was for you to make our marriage work—because I sure as hell wasn't going to. I just assumed everything would fall into place.' His eyes fixed on her face. 'I was wrong.'

'We were both wrong!' she raged back at him.

His hands dropped to his sides and he let out a ragged breath. 'I thought it'd be easy.'

He frowned, remembering how inadequate he'd felt. How lonely too—for he'd been too proud to admit his problems to anyone.

'Only it *wasn't*. And when it got hard I blamed you. I pushed you away,' he said quietly. 'I'm the one that ruined everything, *pireni*! I hurt you and I lied to you, and because of my arrogance and stubborn pride I let you go when I should have done everything in my power to make you stay. And then I had to lie to both my families. All my grandmother wanted was to see me happily married before she died, and I messed that up too.'

His voice cracked and he lowered his head.

'I never meant to hurt you, Prudence. You have to believe me. I just wanted it to be perfect.'

Feeling tears prick the backs of her eyes, Prudence shook her head. 'I know,' she said softly. 'And I don't blame you for what happened.'

Her throat tightened. It was no wonder he'd reacted so badly when their marriage had seemed to falter.

Reaching out, she took his hand and squeezed it. 'You know this morning, when you said we're more alike than we thought? You were right. Our parents' marriages influenced us way too much.' She laughed weakly. 'I actually think it was some kind of miracle that we even got together in the first place.'

Gripping his hand, she dragged him across the room.

'Listen to me, Laszlo!' She picked up the photo,

brandishing it like a weapon. 'I've spent years looking at photos, paintings and sketches. And it's true what they say: every picture *does* tell a story. And this is *their* story. Not yours.'

She put the frame down carefully.

'I don't have a photo of you, but if I did it would tell me your story. The story of a young man who made some mistakes but who is loyal and devoted to his family and who has learned to forgive and trust.' Her eyes flared. 'You haven't let *anyone* down. Your parents' marriage may have looked easy from the outside, but you only knew them as a child. And I'm sorry that your grandmother didn't know about our marriage, but you made her very happy, Laszlo. And you took care of her— just like you're taking care of Janos now.'

He caught hold of her arm and pulled her tightly into his arms, burying his face in her hair. 'I don't deserve you,' he murmured.

For a long, long time, he just held her, his warm breath on her neck. Then at last, he sighed.

'Talking is so tiring. How do women do so much of it?'

She pulled back slightly and smiled up at him. 'We *are* the stronger sex,' she said quietly.

He nodded, his face serious. 'Stronger. Wiser.

You're probably the wisest woman I've ever met, Prudence Elliot. The most beautiful. Most compassionate. Most forgiving.' He sighed again.

'If only I could make a proper Hungarian goulash I'd be perfect,' she said shakily.

He smiled weakly. 'I've had enough of perfection. I'm happy with what I've got.'

Standing on tiptoe, she pressed her mouth against his. 'Me too!'

He kissed her back fiercely and then, groaning, broke away from her. 'You know, all that talk about goulash has made me think about food again. How about we go downstairs and show Rosa where she's been going wrong all these years?'

Later, lying with Prudence curled against his body, Laszlo felt strangely calm. He'd told her everything, and she'd listened while he talked. Not once had she judged him. Instead she'd given him the courage to face his fear. A fear that had chafed at him for so long and corroded his relationship with the only woman he'd ever loved.

Closing his eyes, he felt his heart contract almost painfully.

The woman he still loved. His wife.

His hand tightened around her body and he was

suddenly close to tears, for he had so nearly lost her again. And then he almost laughed out loud as he remembered their teasing conversation of earlier. For he was the one who was trapped in the tower, and *she* had rescued *him*.

Abruptly, he felt his chest grow tight. And then, like a balloon popping, his happiness burst. His relationship with Prudence would soon be over and all his thoughts of love and marriage were just speculation and hope. At no time had Prudence even hinted that she wanted to give their relationship another chance.

He frowned. Come to that matter, he hadn't either.

In fact, he'd made it pretty clear that their relationship was nothing more than a cathartic fling that would terminate at the same time as her period of employment at the castle.

Opening his eyes, he stared bitterly at the photograph of his parents. He needed to show Prudence he'd changed. Words wouldn't be enough this time. But, having convinced her that all he wanted was a loveless affair, how was he going to persuade her that he wanted to give their marriage another chance?

CHAPTER TEN

'ARE YOU READY?'

Laszlo's voice drifted up the stairs, causing Prudence to glance in dismay at the discarded clothes strewn across her bed. So far she was wearing only her underwear and her shoes.

'Nearly!' she called out quickly.

'Nearly? How is that possible? You've been up there for hours...' His voice trailed off as he stepped through the doorway. 'Nice dress,' he said slowly. 'Where's the rest of it?'

She glared at him. 'This isn't the dress. It goes underneath.'

His eyes slid over the sheath of satin.

'And what goes underneath that?' he murmured softly.

'Nothing. That's the point.'

He grinned. 'It's a very good point. Very convincing, in fact.' He walked across the room and kissed the corner of her mouth. 'Although if you took it off I think your point might be clearer still.'

He pulled her towards him and kissed the soft hollow at the base of her neck.

She looked into his eyes and gave him a teasing smile. 'Really? You don't think it might be a little risqué for the party?'

She squirmed against him and he looked down at her, his gaze darkening.

'Hell, yeah! I'm the only person who gets to see you naked,' he growled, lowering his mouth onto hers and kissing her fiercely.

Head spinning, Prudence clung to him, feeling heat—scorching, dizzying heat—wash over her. Just as she thought her legs would give way, she heard him swear softly under his breath.

Groaning, he broke the kiss and released her. 'I can't believe we have to go to this damn party. I've already spent all day with my family.'

He stopped and stared incredulously at the pile of clothes on the bed.

'You're not going to say you don't have anything to wear, are you?' he said slowly.

'No. Yes. I don't know... It depends.'

He frowned. 'On what? What about the dress you chose in Budapest?'

She bit her lip. 'I did get a dress. Only now I'm not sure if it's more of an evening one than party.'

Laszlo winced. 'Can't it be both? We *are* going to an evening party, after all.' His eyes lit up hopefully. 'If you're really worried then maybe we should just stay here?'

Smiling, she shook her head. 'Nice try! But we're not bailing. What would your family think?' She frowned. 'I don't know why you don't want to go anyway.'

Throwing himself down onto the bed, he pushed the dresses to one side and pulled a pillow behind his head. 'Because I want to stay *here*,' he said sulkily. 'And, as it's taken you nearly two hours *not* to get ready, I think the party will probably be ending by the time you're dressed.'

Laughing, Prudence picked up a scarf from the back of a chair and threw it at him. 'It's easy for men!' she said, reaching round and sweeping her long blonde hair into a loose topknot. 'They just put on a suit!' Glancing at him, she felt her smile fade and gave a small cry of exasperation. 'Only you're not!'

Winding the scarf around his neck, he looked up at her calmly. 'Not what?'

'Wearing a suit!'

Looking down at his jeans and shirt, Laszlo frowned. 'What's wrong with this?'

She glowered at him crossly. 'You're joking, aren't you? Laszlo! I thought you said everyone was dressing up?'

He shrugged. 'They are. And I *have* dressed up; this is the shirt I bought yesterday. Anyway, it's my party—I can wear what I like.' Reaching out, he grabbed her hand and pulled her next to him on the bed. 'What's wrong?' he said gently.

'I don't want to let you down in front of your family.'

'How could you ever let me down? If it hadn't been for you I might never have gone through with being Pavel's godfather.' He pressed her hand to his lips and kissed it tenderly. 'Besides, you'd look beautiful wearing that rug.' He glanced at the riotously patterned Afghan carpet on the floor and grimaced.

Stroking his hair off his forehead, she smiled weakly. 'They won't be looking at me anyway. You're the godfather, remember?' Her eyes grew soft and misty. 'The very handsome, very serious godfather.' She hesitated. 'I'm so proud of you.'

He pressed his thumb against her cheekbone. 'You're a good person,' he said softly, leaning forward so that his warm breath tickled her throat. 'Good enough to eat.'

His words excited her unbearably, and she could feel heat pooling between her thighs. Cheeks burning, she gritted her teeth, trying to stay calm. 'You don't want to spoil your appetite. And I need to get dressed,' she said lightly.

He sighed. 'I still don't really get why you're so worried, *pireni*. Although I suppose I'd probably feel the same if I was in your shoes.'

Summoning up a smile, Prudence looked down at her high-heeled black court shoes. 'If you were in my shoes I think you'd bring the party to a standstill!'

He grinned. 'Don't tempt me!'

His eyes met hers and she felt a shiver of desire run over her skin as Laszlo ran his hand slowly up her leg and then abruptly rolled to the other side of the bed.

'You know what? I don't care what you wear.' He groaned. 'But you *have* to put some clothes on or I won't be responsible for what happens.' He stood up. 'In fact, just to be on the safe side, I'm going to go back to the castle. If I put a couple of fields and metre-thick stone walls between us I might just be able to keep my hands off you until after the party!'

He paused and pulled her scarf more tightly around his neck.

'Oh, and I *might* change into something that's a bit more "evening and party wear"!'

She giggled and their eyes met.

'I'll be back to pick you up later…ish.' Blowing her a kiss, he grimaced and shook his head. 'The things we do for love!'

After he'd gone, she spent at least ten minutes mulling over his words. Finally she roused herself. It was just a phrase—a jokey remark that people used all the time. She would be crazy to read anything more into it.

Twenty minutes later she slid a lipstick across her lips and stared critically at her reflection in the dressing table mirror.

She turned her head from side to side. The neckline was perhaps a little lower than she'd normally wear, and her pinned-up hair would probably not survive the dancing, but overall she was satisfied. Still staring at her reflection, she bit her lip. She seemed to be looking at two separate versions of herself. One was serene and cool, the deep smoky grey of the long silk dress highlighting her classic English rose skin and fair hair. The other Prudence was visible only in her eyes, which were dark, apprehensive. Aroused by Laszlo's imagined response to her transformation.

She heard a knock at the door and felt a stab of excitement. *Laszlo!*

Heart pounding, she opened the door—and took a step backwards, her hand over her mouth. He looked impossibly handsome in a classic black dinner jacket, his snowy white shirt unbuttoned at the neck, bow tie hanging loose around the collar.

'It—it's a dinner jacket,' she stammered.

He glanced down at himself nonchalantly. 'This old thing? I found it at the back of my wardrobe,' he murmured.

He smiled, his teeth gleaming in the darkness. She saw the flare of approval and desire in his face and felt her body respond.

'You're beautiful, Prudence,' he said softly. Reaching out, he tugged gently at a tendril of honey-coloured hair, shaping the curl between his fingers. 'I love your hair up like this. You're like a goddess—an Aphrodite.'

Prudence stared at him breathlessly. He was more beautiful than any god she could name. And sexier too, with his shirt open and his eyes dark and teasing.

'That would explain why I can't ever seem to get

warm. I should really be on some hot Greek moun-
tain,' she said lightly, her heart banging against
her chest.

He studied her in silence. 'Speaking of cold…
are you going to invite me in or shall I just wait
out here?'

She blushed. 'Sorry. Of course—come in. I just
need to get my bag.'

Shutting the door behind him, Laszlo pulled off
his jacket and hung it carelessly over the back of
the sofa. He sat down in one of the armchairs,
picked up a magazine and began to flick through it.

After a moment he sighed and put his feet up
onto the coffee table. 'What do women put in their
bags anyway?' he said idly.

Prudence smiled. 'All the things men keep in
their jacket pockets. Money, keys, lipstick…'

'I don't have any lipstick,' Laszlo said sadly.

She laughed softly. 'You don't have any money
or keys either.'

Grinning up at her, he tugged her leg and she let
herself fall into his lap.

'Is that so? How would you know? Or have you
been going through my clothes as well as breaking into my house?'

He shook his head and, laughing, she wriggled

free of his hands. Standing up, she pulled down his jacket and began patting the pockets one by one.

'See?' she said triumphantly. 'Empty. Oh—' Her fingers touched something small and rectangular and then suddenly she was holding a small velvet-covered rectangular box.

'What's this?'

Frowning, Laszlo stood up. He paused and then swore softly under his breath. 'Damn it!' He shook his head and then smiled ruefully. 'That was—is actually for you.'

She stared at him, too shocked to speak. 'For me?' she said finally. 'What is it?'

His eyes met hers and he laughed quietly. 'Open it and see!'

Heart pounding, she felt her mind dance forward as she lifted the lid—and then she gasped. 'Oh, Laszlo. It's beautiful.'

He nodded. 'It's to match your eyes.'

She stared at the luminous grey pearl necklace in silence, shivers running up and down her spine. 'It's truly lovely. But I didn't get *you* anything,' she said, looking up at him anxiously.

A dark flush coloured his cheeks. There was a pause, and then he shook his head slowly. 'It's not from me.' He cleared his throat. 'It's from my grandfather. He would have given it to you himself, but he got tied up on the phone and he wanted you to have it before the party.'

Prudence blinked 'Your grandfather?' She swallowed. Her skin felt hot and raw; his gaze was blistering her skin. She felt stupid and naive. Keeping her gaze averted, she breathed in deeply. 'That's so sweet of him. But I can't possibly accept it.'

Laszlo frowned. 'You must. Please. He chose them himself as a thank-you for all your hard work.'

She bit her lip. 'He didn't need to thank me. Not with something as beautiful as this. Shall I wear it tonight?' she said shakily.

Nodding, he reached out and took the necklace gently from her hand. 'It's not as beautiful as you. Now, stand up and turn round!'

She turned away, feeling her skin tingle as his warm fingers slid over her.

'There! Let me see…'

She turned back towards him slowly and lifted her head. Their eyes met and her pupils shrank beneath the intensity of his gaze.

'You don't need any jewellery. Your eyes and lips are your jewels,' he said roughly.

Breathing deeply, he stepped away, his eyes narrowing.

'And now I'd like to give you *my* gift. I'm sorry it doesn't quite match up to my grandfather's.' He smiled ruefully. 'If he'd been any other man I would have punched him on the nose. But what could I do? He's my grandfather!'

'*Your* gift?'

He reached down and pulled a small embellished leather bag from beneath his shirt. 'It's a *putsi*. It means "little pocket". It's traditional for Romany women to carry one.' He looped the cord over his hand and held it out to her.

'It's beautiful,' she croaked.

Her heart was racing, and she knew that her feelings were all over her face, but she was too happy to care. Her whole body felt as though it were filling with light.

With hands that shook slightly, she turned the bag over. It rattled softly. 'Is there something inside it?'

He nodded. 'Amulets. Magic charms.' He shrugged. 'They're supposed to bring good luck. Ward off evil. If you believe in that sort of thing.'

She nodded, unable to speak.

'Just don't open the bag,' he said, deepening his voice dramatically. 'Or the magic will fail.'

Shivering, she looked up with wide, uncertain eyes.

He pulled her towards him, laughing softly. 'I'm kidding. You can open it if you want.'

She began to pull clumsily at the drawstring and then, looking up, saw him watching her. Her fingers faltered.

'I think I'll wait,' she said slowly. 'Save my luck for later.'

Gently, he reached up and stroked her cheek. 'You don't need luck.' He glanced at the soft curve of her waist beneath the clinging silk and frowned. 'But if we don't go right now there's no amulet on earth that's going to stop me ripping that dress off you!'

'I'm ready!' she said hastily.

Reaching down, she picked up her small beaded evening bag, opened it and put the *putsi* inside. Then, looking up, she smiled at him shyly.

'Thank you, Laszlo. I'll keep it close to me always. And I love it just as much as the pearls.'

He watched her coolly, back to his old inscrutable self.

'It's my pleasure. And I'm pleased.' He grinned. 'Utterly unconvinced, but pleased.'

He turned towards the door but she put her hand on his arm. 'Wait!' Their eyes met and then she blushed and pointed to his neck. 'What about your bow tie?'

Glancing down, he frowned. 'Oh…I gave up,' he said simply. 'Papi can do them in his sleep, but he was busy on the phone, and every time I tried to talk to him he shooed me away,' he grumbled.

Their eyes met and she burst out laughing. 'You are *such* a spoilt baby.' She reached out and did up his top button. 'Your grandfather was probably talking to the caterers. Now, lift your chin!' Deftly, Prudence twisted the black silk between her fingers. 'Turn around!' Stepping backwards, she stared at him assessingly. 'Perfect!' she said softly.

He grinned slowly. 'Me? Or the bow tie?'

Rolling her eyes, she picked up the pashmina she'd had the foresight to buy at the airport and slid it over her shoulders. She let out a breath.

Laszlo looked at her enquiringly. 'Ready?'

'No. But do I have a choice?'

He kissed her lightly on the lips. 'Not any more.

Come on! Let's go!' He gave Prudence his arm and, opening the front door, stepped into the night air.

She gave a gasp of surprise, for, leading away as far as the eye could see, hundreds of tiny flickering flares edged the path up to the castle. 'That's so pretty!'

Shaking his head, Laszlo laughed. 'They're supposed to stop us breaking our necks. But I suppose they *do* look a bit like fireflies.' His golden eyes gently mocked her excitement. 'It all adds to the magic of the occasion. For the women and children!'

Prudence laughed. 'Don't make me use my *putsi*,' she said teasingly.

'There's nothing wrong with a bit of magic.' Laszlo grinned. 'I'll remind you of that later, when my Uncle Lajos starts doing conjuring tricks.'

The noise of laughter and music greeted them as they walked along the gravel path towards the barn and Prudence squeezed Laszlo's arm nervously.

She had enjoyed the christening more than she'd expected. The tiny church had been bright with sunlight and filled with flowers. And seeing Laszlo hold Pavel in his arms, his unguarded face still with pride, she could have wept with love and envy. Laszlo's family had been polite and friendly.

But now the darkness felt intimidating, and she suddenly wished that she was walking in as his wife.

Shivering, she pushed the thought away. 'It sounds like the party's already started,' she said quickly. 'How many people are coming?'

Laszlo shrugged. 'I don't know. Probably a hundred—maybe more.'

Prudence felt her feet stutter to a halt. 'A—a *hundred*?' she stammered. 'A hundred people?' She stopped and stared at him incredulously. 'Why didn't you tell me?'

He gazed at her with a maddening lack of concern. 'I thought you knew? Did you think it was just the guests from the christening?' He laughed softly. 'No. This is *everyone*.' Frowning, he took her hand in his. 'Does it matter? I mean, they're all family...'

Swallowing, she smiled weakly. 'Is that why there were more women than men at the church?'

He grinned. 'They didn't all come to the church. A lot of the men think that priests take away your manhood. Mine seems fine, though!' His eyes gleamed in the darkness.

She knew he was teasing her, trying to make her

relax, but she couldn't. Feeling suddenly queasy with panic, Prudence clutched his arm more tightly.

Laszlo gave her hand a comforting squeeze. 'You did the hard part this morning. It'll be fine. They're going to love you. Trust me.'

Trust: how could so much be wrapped up in that one little word? 'Okay.' Heart pounding, she nodded. 'Okay. But you have to trust me too, Laszlo. That's how trust works.'

In the darkness, she couldn't tell if he'd taken in her words or not. She opened her mouth to speak again, and then, behind them, the door to the barn opened and light and noise and colour hit her like a physical blow.

'Laszlo! *Laszlo!*'

Prudence stared in astonishment round the barn. All around her, hands were reaching across and patting Laszlo on the back, pulling him by the arm, calling out his name. Turning towards her, he grinned and shouted back something in Hungarian, or maybe Romany. But the noise in the barn made it impossible for her to do anything but smile and nod.

Children were running around, darting through the crowds of smartly dressed adults, laughing and shouting. Some men dressed in dark suits and waistcoats were singing, stamping in time to guitars, and men and women, old and young, were dancing in a mass of people that seemed to fill one end of the vast barn.

Laszlo guided her into a part of the barn that had been screened off as a cloakroom. He turned to her and grinned. 'Now, *this* is a party. A Romany party!' he whispered in her ear.

She nodded. 'A hundred people?' She glared at him accusingly as he led her back into the main barn. 'There must be well over two hundred!'

He glanced round the room. 'Nearer three, I'd guess.' His eyes were light and teasing.

She shook her head. 'You're incorrigible, Laszlo Cziffra! You knew *exactly* how many people were coming—and I bet you were always going to wear a dinner jacket, weren't you?'

'No.'

His smile sent shivers up and down her spine.

'I was always going to wear a suit. But then I thought tonight was special—'

He turned as a dancing couple barged into him and apologised. She blinked in confusion. What did he mean by 'special'? She felt his hand tighten on hers and looking up, found him watching her, his gaze fierce and glittering.

'We need to talk.'

Wordlessly, she nodded—and then, glancing over his shoulder, she noticed a middle-aged couple watching them curiously.

'Not here,' she murmured, flinching as another couple skimmed past Laszlo's back.

Frowning, he put his arm round her protectively. 'Shall we go outside? It's quieter there… less chance of injury.'

'Yes.' She paused. 'But could we find your grandfather first? I want to thank him for the necklace.'

Laszlo studied her face and then nodded slowly. Scanning over the heads of the dancers, he pointed across the barn. 'He's over there! And there's Mihaly too.' He gripped her hand tightly. 'Don't let go. I don't want to lose you.'

He turned and began to push his way through the crush of people, pulling her behind him. Every few metres he was stopped by guests and Prudence found herself being introduced to a baffling array of people. Finally they reached the other side of the barn, where tables and chairs had been set up and trestles of food and drink lined the walls.

'Laszlo!' Mihaly reached out and yanked his cousin into a crushing embrace. He took a step back and, glancing down at Laszlo's suit, grinned wickedly. 'What's this? They've got you being a waiter at your own party?'

Pushing Laszlo under his arm, he sidestepped in front of Prudence and bowed.

'Miss Elliot! You look beautiful! I wonder, may I have this dance with you?'

He gave a yelp that turned into a laugh as Laszlo grabbed him from behind and punched him on the arm.

'No. You may not!'

Still laughing, Mihaly held out his hand to Prudence. 'Don't listen to him, Miss Elliot.' He gestured towards an elderly woman sitting by the dance floor, a walking frame by her side. 'That's my great-aunt. Laszlo danced with her once! Just *once*!'

He and Laszlo both burst into laughter, but there was no mistaking the possessive note in his voice as Laszlo pulled her against him. 'Prudence won't be dancing with anyone but me. And *you're* going to need a walking frame too, cousin, if you don't back off!'

Trying to ignore the warm rush of pleasure at his words, she glanced anxiously over to where Janos was talking to another elderly man. 'I must just speak to your grandfather,' she said quietly.

Janos broke off his conversation as she approached him. He smiled warmly. 'You look quite lovely, my dear.'

Prudence blushed. 'Thank you so much, Janos. It's such a beautiful necklace.' Standing on tiptoe, she reached up and kissed Janos gently on the cheek.

Smiling, he patted her on the hand. 'It's my pleasure.' He glanced over Prudence's shoulder to where Laszlo and Mihaly were still fooling around with each other. Sighing, he shook his head. 'They act like children when they get together, but it's nice for me to see Laszlo having fun.'

His face clouded.

'I know it must appear to you that he's had a charmed life, living here in a castle surrounded by priceless works of art. But he's known a great deal of unhappiness,' he said quietly. 'He's seen so much sickness and death and grief.' He smiled sadly. 'Of course I love having my grandson live with me, but he's spent far too much of his life cooped up in the castle with me.'

He hesitated.

'We're too shut off here. It's made him push away the world. Turn away from life itself. But you coming here has changed that. He seems so much happier.'

Prudence blushed. 'I don't think I can really take the credit for that.' She swallowed. 'But I'm glad he's happy. He deserves to be. Even though he's so incredibly annoying and stubborn…' Her mouth twisted. 'I don't think I know anyone quite like him!'

Janos burst out laughing. 'Nothing you can't handle, I imagine?'

She laughed. 'No. I think we've pretty much worked out our differences.' Biting her lip, she hesitated. 'But I think it's not just Laszlo who's changed. You've changed too.'

Janos nodded. 'Yes. I have.' His eyes flickered with excitement. 'And there may be more changes to come. But none of it would have happened without your hard work and patience.'

Prudence glanced down to the necklace gleaming at her throat. 'Hmm… Pearls for patience? I think I should quit while I'm ahead.'

Janos smiled. 'It's a fair exchange! And happily Laszlo actually remembered to give you the necklace.' He frowned. 'I wasn't entirely sure he would. He can be a little forgetful.'

'Jakob's not forgetful!' Laszlo slid between his

grandfather and Prudence. 'What are you talking about, Papi? He's got an excellent memory. Or were you casting aspersions on *me*?' He smiled mischievously at Janos, who shook his head and began to speak in Hungarian.

For a long moment Laszlo said nothing. His expression didn't change, but something in his gaze seemed to reach out to her—she could almost feel his hands on her skin, even though they were standing apart.

Finally both men nodded and then, his face softening, Laszlo held out his hand. 'Dance with me?'

Prudence felt the air squeeze from her lungs and for a moment time seemed to stop—and then slowly she smiled.

The rest of the party passed with unconscionable speed. Later, Prudence would try to piece the evening together. She had danced and eaten, and talked until her voice was hoarse from trying to compete with the music. And then finally the music had slowed and the lights had dimmed and Laszlo had held her tightly against him. They'd danced until suddenly Janos had been there, telling them that he was tired and was going to go home to bed.

'I'll walk you home, Papi. I could do with some

fresh air,' Laszlo said, pulling his dinner jacket from the back of a chair. He turned to Prudence, his eyes locking onto hers. 'Shall I come back for you?' he asked quietly.

She shook her head. 'No. I'll come now.'

Smiling, he slipped his jacket over her shoulders, and together the three of them walked up to the castle.

Inside the hall, Janos turned and frowned.

'Are you all right, Papi?' Laszlo stared at his grandfather.

'Oh, I'm fine. The fresh air's just woken me up.' Janos hesitated. 'I wonder… Do either of you feel up to a nightcap?'

Glancing at one another, they both nodded simultaneously.

Janos beamed. 'Wonderful. Let's go and warm up.'

In the study, a fire was flickering in the grate. Laszlo leant over and banged the glowing logs with a poker, and flames leapt up as though defending themselves.

'Sit down by the fire, Papi. Prudence—come here,' he ordered.

Janos sat down and glanced apologetically around the room. 'I'm afraid I may have been a little disingenuous.' He smoothed an imaginary crease from his trouser leg. 'You see, I have something I want to discuss with you both. I was going to wait until tomorrow...' Lifting his head, he frowned. 'But it's been playing on my mind.'

Prudence looked down at her hands in her lap, feeling Laszlo's gaze on the side of her face.

'So? What is it, Papi?'

Janos paused. He looked alert and animated, the vigour in his eyes belying his age. 'I'm thinking about making some changes. And I'd be quite interested in hearing what you think.'

Laszlo raised his eyebrows. 'Not the moat again, Papi?' he said slowly.

Janos shook his head and gave a reluctant smile. 'No. Not the moat. Although it *does* have something to do with the castle.' Pausing, he glanced across at Prudence. 'It was you, my dear girl, who gave me the idea.'

Prudence gaped at him. 'I did?' she said incredulously.

There was a moment's silence, and then Laszlo cleared his throat. 'So. Don't keep us in suspense, then, Papi. What's the big idea?'

Smiling, Janos shook his head. 'You're just like your mother. Always so impatient.' He looked up at his grandson, his expression tender and hope-ful. 'All my life I've been surrounded by beauty. Now I'd like to share my good fortune with other people.' He paused again, his eyes bright, almost feverish with excitement. 'And that's why I want to turn the castle into a museum.'

CHAPTER ELEVEN

THERE WAS A stunned silence in the room. Finally Laszlo shook his head. 'I'm sorry. Did you just say you wanted to turn the castle into a *museum*?' He gave his grandfather a long, searching look. 'Why on earth would you want to do that?'

Janos raised his hands placatingly. 'To give something back, Laszlo.'

Laszlo frowned. 'You *do* give something back. Quite a lot of "something", if that last meeting we had with the accountants is anything to go by.'

Janos shook his head. 'Yes. I give to charity. But this would be different.'

His frown darkening, Laszlo began pacing the room. 'Different?' He gave a short laugh. 'It would definitely be *different*. And disruptive—and intrusive. Have you really thought what it would be like to have a bunch of people wandering about in our home?' Stopping in front of his grandfather, he stubbed the carpet with the toe of his shoe. 'I just don't understand why you would want to do this. And why now?'

He shot Prudence a questioning glance.

'*Is* this something to do with you? What did you say to him?'

She stared at him, confused. 'I—I don't know—' she stammered.

Reaching out, Janos patted the chair beside him. 'Laszlo! *Laszlo!* Sit down. Prudence and I were talking about her life in England and she mentioned the Soane's Museum. That's all.'

Prudence watched as Laszlo allowed his grandfather to pull him into the chair.

Janos frowned. 'I'm so sorry.' He glanced at Prudence apologetically. 'I should have waited until tomorrow. We're probably too tired and emotional after the party to be having this sort of conversation.' His voice trembled. 'It was thoughtless of me. I suppose I've just had this idea buzzing around my head for so long now that I forgot it would be new and shocking to you.' He sighed. 'And I just wanted to share it with you both.'

Taking his grandfather's hand, Laszlo squeezed it hard. He looked so young and troubled that Prudence turned away.

'I'm sorry, Papi,' she heard him say softly. 'Of

course I want to share your idea. I just wasn't ex-pecting it.' He smiled weakly. 'But I want to hear all about it. So—how will it all work?'

Janos smiled back at him. 'It's not going to hap-pen overnight. Someone from the Museums Com-mittee is coming over in a couple of weeks, to take a look at what we've got here, and then I think there will be a lot of long but necessary meetings. Quite possibly the castle will be ready for visitors by the end of next year.'

Laszlo nodded slowly. 'And how will that work? I mean having visitors. You're not expecting me to give guided tours or anything?' He spoke lightly but his face had tightened.

Laughing, Janos shook his head. 'No, Laszlo. You won't be giving tours around the castle. We won't have much to do with the visitors at all.'

Laszlo frowned. 'Given that they'll be wander-ing around our home, I think we *will*.'

There was a long, strained pause and then Janos coughed. 'The castle won't *be* our home when it's a museum, Laszlo. By the time it opens to the pub-lic we'll have moved out.'

'Moved out?' Laszlo said slowly. 'Moved out of the castle?' He shook his head. 'Papi... What are you talking about? This is your home. *Our* home. It's been in our family for hundreds of years!'

'I know—and I love this castle. It's been an enormous privilege to own such an incredible building. But, my darling boy, it's not a home any more.' He put his hands on his grandson's shoulders and said roughly, 'This castle is a museum in everything but name. And we both need to accept that and move on.'

For a moment the room hummed with a silence that was broken only by the spitting of the fire, and then finally Laszlo nodded.

'I know,' he said quietly. 'I suppose it's just that it's taken me a long time to think of it as home and now—' He cleared his throat. 'But you're right. It's ridiculous, the two of us rattling around here like this.' He managed a small smile. 'Have you told Rosa yet?'

Shaking his head, Janos frowned. 'Not yet. I wanted to speak to you first.' He screwed up his face. 'I must admit I'm a little worried about telling her.'

Laszlo pursed his lips. 'She'll be fine once she gets used to the idea.' He smiled. 'And as long as she gets to fuss around *you* she'll be happy wherever she lives.' Looking up at his grandfather, he hesitated. 'Which sort of brings me to my next question… Where exactly are you planning on us living?'

Janos let out a breath. 'That would rather depend on Prudence.'

Prudence felt her fingers curl painfully around her glass as both men turned to stare at her. 'M-me? Why does it depend on *me*?' she stammered.

'Because I was rather hoping that after the cataloguing is complete you might consider staying on,' Janos said gently. 'That's why I want you to be here now. So I can ask you if you would like to be the museum's curator.'

Prudence stared at him speechlessly. Stay on? In Hungary? With Laszlo?

Finally, she found her voice. 'I—I'm not…I don't know what to say…' she faltered.

Janos laughed. 'Of course you don't. How could you? Please don't look so worried, Prudence. I'm not expecting you to give me an answer right now,' he said hastily. 'I'm just hoping you might think about it over the next few days. Or weeks. Take as long as you like.'

Heart pounding, Prudence gave a weak smile. 'Thank you. And thank you for thinking of me,' she said slowly.

Janos laughed. 'My dear, I didn't think of any-one else.' He frowned. 'I must confess before you came I was quite worried about how everything would work. You know—having a stranger in our home. But you coming here has been a blessing.' He glanced across to Laszlo, his lined face creas-ing into a smile. 'And you're part of our family now—isn't she, Laszlo?'

Almost intoxicated by hope and longing, Pru-dence glanced across at Laszlo—and her bub-bling happiness began to ebb away. For, meeting his gaze, she saw from his face that he shared none of her pleasure or excitement.

She felt panic clutch at her chest as he stared at her in silence, smiling unsteadily, a strange, un-familiar light glittering in his eyes.

Abruptly he stood up and cleared his throat. 'I'm going to go back to the party. Make sure every-thing's okay. And you need to get some sleep, Papi. It's been a very long night for you. And this can wait until morning. We don't want to push Miss Elliot into a decision she regrets.'

Her body tensed as he turned, but he didn't even look at her as he walked out of the room. Pain and panic tore through her as she watched him leave. For one terrible, agonising moment she wanted to go after him and pull him back. Demand that he stay and explain. But she stopped herself. Laszlo had never been much good with words, but on this occasion he didn't need to be. He didn't need to explain anything. His actions were loud enough.

He didn't want her to stay.

He didn't want her at all.

It was nearly time to leave. The *vardo* gleamed in the late-morning sun. Gently Prudence ran her hand over the gold-painted scrolls and garlands and bouquets of flowers. It was truly a labour of love. For the craftsman who'd made it, at least. She bit her lip.

Slowly she walked up the steps, touching, feeling the wood smooth and warm beneath her fingers. Picking up a pillow from the bed, she closed her eyes and inhaled: woodsmoke and orange blossom. It was his scent, but even as she inhaled it seemed to fade. Opening her eyes, she crawled onto the bed and stared bleakly out of the window. From where she lay the castle seemed to fill the tiny square of glass entirely, blocking out the light.

Just as Laszlo had dominated her life from the moment she'd met him seven years ago.

Rolling onto her back, she closed her eyes.

They had come so close to making it work.

Yesterday, for the first time ever, he had opened up to her about so many things. His family…his fears. Her breath caught in her throat. He had needed her emotionally—wanted her support. And she had let herself believe that it meant something, for it had felt as if something had changed between them. As if there had been some shift in the fundament of their relationship.

Her heart gave a painful lurch. But of course, as with so much of their relationship, nothing was what it seemed.

She shivered, remembering Laszlo's face when Janos had called her one of the family. She could have ignored his reaction. Let it go. As she'd let so many other things go because she'd feared losing him. But she didn't fear losing him any more.

On the contrary—what she'd feared most was that she wouldn't be strong enough to leave him.

Her eyes grew hot and damp. It had been so, so hard the last time. She drew in a breath. But she had got over it eventually. And she would do so again. In time, and with distance between them. Which was why she'd gone to find Janos that morning and told him that she needed to go home for a few days. She'd used the excuse that she needed to talk through his offer with Edmund and he'd agreed immediately, as she'd known he would. Jakob had even pulled strings so that a seat had been found for her on a plane leaving that evening.

Opening her eyes, she covered her mouth with her hand, trying to hold back her misery. Part of her wanted to stay. The part that felt as if it was disintegrating. But what would be the point? Her love wasn't enough for Laszlo; *she* wasn't enough for him.

She lifted her chin and the knot of misery in her stomach began to loosen. She was not about to crumble. Laszlo might not love her but she still had her self-respect. And if she wanted to avoid the same fate as her mother, diminished and worn down by unrequited love, she needed to get away from him.

That meant leaving Hungary. And never coming back.

It was the first time she'd acknowledged that fact—if not out loud then in her head. But she knew it was the right—the only choice she had. She needed to be where her judgement wasn't skewed by her heart. That was why she was going home to her family.

She glanced up at the sky and frowned. And why she needed to start packing.

Back at the cottage, suitcase packed, she walked dully from room to room, checking for anything she might have forgotten. With a stab of pain she noticed Laszlo's dinner jacket, hanging on the back of the kitchen door. He'd draped it over her shoulders when they'd left the party and she'd still been wearing it later when, dumb and still shivering from shock, she had let Janos get Gregor, the handyman and chauffeur, to escort her back to the cottage.

She lifted her chin. She would give it to him at lunchtime. Despite eating breakfast at the cottage, she'd resigned herself to the fact that seeing him one last time was inevitable. At least with Janos there there would be no risk of her losing control and throwing a bowl of soup in his face.

But at lunchtime Laszlo's seat was conspicuously empty.

Janos was apologetic. 'He didn't come down for breakfast either. He's probably with Mihaly,' he said, trying to sound encouraging as Prudence tried and failed to eat the delicious lunch Rosa had made especially for her. 'I'm sure he'll be here any moment.'

But he hadn't appeared.

Later, waiting at the airport, she felt almost sick with nerves, for part of her had stupidly hoped that he would come after her.

It was only when she was boarding the plane that she knew that it was really, finally over.

Glancing wearily out of the window, she watched the patchwork of green and brown fields disappear beneath the clouds. It was better that it had ended like this, with her on her own. There would be nothing to haunt her now, for that last evening in Janos's study seemed to have fled her memory.

Outside, everything had turned white, and she felt something like peace slide over her. For even though it had been hard to leave, and it was going to be much, much harder to learn to live without him again, she didn't regret what had happened. Finally she could accept that she and Laszlo would never have a future together. And, more importantly, she'd learned that there was nothing to fear from the past: her mother's choices did not have to be hers.

She had the power to shape her life. Finally, she could face the future without fear or regret.

She shivered. Closing her eyes, she shrugged her coat over her body. But that was the future—right now she just wanted to get warm. Only, huddling into her jacket, she doubted she would ever feel warm again…

Staring at the museum's sprinklers longingly, Prudence sighed. If only she could set them off… But, even though it was her last day at work, she couldn't imagine herself ruining hundreds of priceless artefacts in exchange for one blissfully cool shower.

She scowled. London was in the grip of an Indian summer and she was sick of the heat. Tucking a strand of limp hair behind her ear, she took a breath of warm air and began to speak.

'And this is the cast of the Belvedere Apollo.' Gesturing to the statue in front of her, Prudence turned to the crowd of tourists gathered expectantly around her and smiled. 'It's a copy made for Lord Burlington in Italy, sometime around 1719. Before it came to the museum it was held at Chiswick House.'

She paused and glanced around at the faces staring up at her. Since leaving Seymour's she had been working part-time at the museum, and although she'd enjoyed it she was looking forward to leaving. These people were her last tour group. And after that—

She bit her lip. After that she'd take it one day at a time. What was important was that Daisy and Edmund had been so understanding and so supportive. About everything. And, although she would of course like to get a place of her own, she had agreed to keep on living with them for the immediate future.

She looked up and took a breath. 'The Belvedere Apollo takes its name from the Belvedere Palace in the Vatican, where it has resided since the early fifteen-hundreds. The sculpture depicts the Greek god Apollo as an archer. He is nude except for his sandals and a robe slung over his shoulders.'

Pausing, she took another breath. It felt hotter than Greece in the museum, and suddenly she remembered the crisp, cold mornings in Hungary. For a fraction of a second, her smile faltered but, gripping her clipboard tightly, she ploughed on.

'That concludes our tour this morning. If you have any questions, please don't hesitate to ask. I hope you enjoy the rest of your visit to the museum and your stay in London. Thank you.'

Picking up her handbag from behind the desk, she walked towards the hallway, where the air conditioning greeted her like a fridge door opening. Fanning her face, she sat down and closed her eyes.

'Excuse me?'

For a moment, her brain was in free fall and then her eyes flew open as she thought she recognised his voice. But it couldn't be him, could it? Why would Laszlo be in London? He hadn't even bothered to say goodbye.

The sun was in her eyes. At first she could make out only a blurred dark shape. But then she saw his outline, and the breath seemed to freeze in her throat.

He stepped out of the light and she felt her legs slide away from under her.

He caught her as she fell.

'Here…'

She felt his hands, warm and firm, guide her into a seat. Her head was spinning.

'Drink this.'

Water from the water cooler. So cold and fresh it might have come from one of the streams that criss-crossed the fields around his castle.

She moaned and Laszlo crouched down by her side, holding a glass to her lips.

'Just sip it.'

The noise of traffic surged into the room as downstairs a door was opened.

'Are you okay, Miss Elliot?' Now Joe, the doorman, was leaning over her. 'Do you want me to get a doctor?'

She shook her head. 'No. Thank you.'

And then Laszlo stood up, his body screening her from Joe's anxious face. 'I've got it from here.'

He spoke pleasantly, but some alarm must have shown on her face, for Joe stood his ground. 'And you are, sir…?'

'I'm her husband!'

There was a tense silence, and then she heard Joe's feet retreating across the tiled floor.

She was suddenly furious. 'What are you doing here?'

He ignored her question. 'Finish your water.'

'Answer my question!' She glared at him.

He studied her impassively. 'I will. After you've finished the water.'

Swallowing her anger first, she drained the cup and handed it to him. 'Now answer my question!'

'Surely you should be answering *my* questions? After all, you *do* work here.'

She stared at him in disbelief and then, reaching up, pulled her name badge off her shirt and dropped it in the bin. 'Not any more!' She glared at him and then abruptly stood up. 'Goodbye, Laszlo!' she said quietly. 'I hope you enjoy the rest of your visit to the museum and your stay in London.'

He regarded her calmly and then, as she took a step forward, moved in front of her.

She shot him a frustrated glance. 'Could you move, please?'

He stood silently in front of her and she shook her head and looked away from him. 'You can stand there all day if you want. I'm used to silent men made of stone.' Her hands clenched at her sides. 'But it won't change anything. I have nothing left to say to you.'

He waited until finally, reluctantly, she turned to face him. 'Quite a lot to write, though, it would appear,' he said. 'About ending our marriage.'

She watched wordlessly as he reached into his pocket and pulled out an envelope. Her skin was suddenly tight across her face and she felt cornered. And then she met his gaze, for she wasn't going to let him intimidate her.

'What about it?' she said shortly. 'I told you in Hungary that I wanted a divorce. I still do. There's no point leaving things as they are.'

'And how *are* things?' His voice was hoarse. 'You see, I thought you were happy.'

She shook her head in exasperation. 'I was. I *am*. But when did my happiness matter to you, Laszlo? You only care about yourself, and you didn't look too happy when your grandfather asked me to stay on as curator. Or when he called me one of the family.'

She felt a stab of pain at the memory and suddenly could barely see his face through her tears.

'In fact, you were so happy you walked off.'

His face tightened. Running his hand through his hair, he said slowly, 'I didn't want you to—'

'Didn't want me to stay. I know—'

'No.' He cut her off. 'I didn't want my grandfather to rush you. You seemed unsure, and he was so desperate for you to agree. I thought he'd just keep on pushing and—'

'And you thought I'd say yes?' Her voice rose and she shook her head. 'So you decided to talk it over with me and your grandfather.' She paused, her lip curling contemptuously. 'Oh, no. You *didn't*. You walked out.'

Laszlo looked at her, his expression bleak. Finally he nodded. 'Yes. I walked away. I didn't know what else to do. So much had happened between us, but so much still wasn't resolved. Like us being married. I knew if you agreed to take the job then you'd come back. And not just for a couple of weeks this time.'

Prudence felt like throwing up. 'Imagine that,' she said flatly. 'No *wonder* you couldn't wait to get away.'

She took a painful breath as he shook his head.

'I wasn't thinking about me. I knew *you'd* have a problem with that.'

Staring at him incredulously, she gave a humourless laugh. 'Not as big a problem as you.' Pausing, she gritted her teeth. 'I don't really understand what you're trying to say, Laszlo. But you know what? I don't care any more.'

'I do!'

He practically shouted the words and she took a step back from him.

'I care. And I cared in Hungary. You *hated* lying to my grandfather about us. And I knew it would be a problem doing it again. And for so long. I thought if he pushed you, you'd panic and say no—'

His voice cracked and she stared at him in shock. 'And I didn't want you to.'

For a moment she thought she must have misheard him. She opened her mouth and then closed it again. Her breath was burning her throat. 'Why?' she said shakily. 'Why didn't you want me to say no?'

He stared at her and then bowed his head. 'Because I love you.'

Her heart twisted inside her. 'Don't say that, Laszlo.'

Tears sprang to her eyes as he reached out and, taking her hands, raised them to his lips.

'I *will* say it.'

He looked up and she saw that his face was wet with tears.

'I will say it. And I'll keep on saying it until you believe me. I love you. I only worked it out when we talked about my parents and their marriage, and I realised that I'd only believed in *their* love and not mine.' He grimaced. 'I should have just come right out and told you, but…' He smiled weakly. 'I'm so bad at this stuff.'

He shook his head.

'I have trouble explaining it to myself. Let alone to the person I'm so scared of losing.'

She stared at him in exasperation. 'So you thought it would be a good idea to make me believe that our relationship was only about sex?'

'I'm an idiot.'

'So it wasn't?'

He screwed up his face. 'Maybe a little bit—at the beginning. When I was angry and mean.' He let out a ragged sigh. 'But I'm only flesh and blood, and I don't think you have any idea how sexy you looked in that blouse and skirt and those heels.'

He bit his lip.

'But it changed. *I* changed. I wanted more. I wanted my wife back! I was going to tell you before the party but I bottled out.' Letting go of her hand, he sighed. 'If only I'd let you open the *putsi* when you wanted to,' he said sadly.

Prudence reached into her handbag and pulled out the small leather bag that she hadn't been able to face discarding.

He stared at it as though mesmerised. 'Open it!'

His voice was husky and she pulled clumsily at the cord. With shaking fingers she tipped the bag upside down and into her hand tumbled an acorn, a key and a beautiful diamond ring.

She felt suddenly faint again. But this time with happiness. 'Oh, Laszlo!' she whispered.

'Prudence—' He reached out hesitantly and, taking the ring from her hand, slid it onto her finger.

'I thought you didn't want me,' she said, tears rolling over her cheeks.

He stepped close to her and took her hands in his. 'And I thought you didn't want *me*.' His voice cracked. 'After the party I went to Mihaly and I told him everything.' He clenched his teeth. 'He told me to stop being such an idiot and tell you how I felt.' He smiled ruefully. 'Actually, he didn't quite use those words. They were slightly more colourful.'

Prudence laughed.

His smile faded. 'But when I got back to the castle you'd gone.' He took a breath. 'Then I lost it and I told my grandfather everything as well.'

Prudence bit her lip. 'And…?'

Frowning, Laszlo pulled her closer. 'He told me I was an idiot too.'

She pulled away slightly and smiled. 'I wish I'd stayed after all,' she said teasingly. There was a brief silence, and then she said hesitantly, 'Were they angry?'

Laszlo shook his head. 'No. They were delighted. In fact, I think they thought I was quite lucky to catch you. And they love you already. Almost as much as I do.' His face tightened, grew suddenly strained. 'I just wish my grandmother was here.

She so wanted to see me married and with a family of my own.'

He gave her an unsteady smile.

'I'm warning you now. You think my grandfather was pushy about you taking the curator's job? Just wait until my aunts hear that I'm married!'

'Never mind your aunts. What about *you*? Do you want children?'

He grinned. 'Yeah, I do. Loads. At least seven.'

'Seven?' she squeaked.

He nodded, suddenly serious. 'One for every year we were apart,' he murmured, tightening his grip around her waist.

She smiled. 'I see. I suppose we should get started, then?'

He grinned. 'Definitely! I'd like to be a father as soon as possible. Like in about nine months. Do you think that's possible?'

She kissed him gently on the lips. 'I can do it in seven.'

He looked at her blankly. 'Seven? You mean nine.'

In reply, she took his hand and put it gently on her stomach. 'No. I mean seven.'

He stared down at the slight bump of her belly. 'Really?'

She nodded. 'Really!'

Pulling her gently into his arms, he closed his eyes, too choked to speak. 'Only another six to go,' he whispered against her cheek—and then abruptly, he released her and took a step back, his face clouding over.

'What is it?' She stared at him anxiously.

He let out a long breath. 'Everything moved pretty fast after you left. Papi and Rosa have moved into the cottage, but...' He frowned. 'As of tomorrow I'm going to be homeless.'

'Oh,' she said slowly. 'Actually, this really is my last day at work. So, as of now, I'm unemployed.'

They stared at each other in silence, and then both of them burst out laughing.

'For better for worse,' he said softly.

She felt his gaze drift over her face. 'For richer for poorer!' she murmured.

He grinned, and then his smile faded. 'Don't worry. I'm not going to make you live in a trailer.'

'I don't mind—' she began, but he shook his head, grimacing.

'No. But I do.' A faint flush coloured his cheeks. 'I know I shouldn't really say it, but I don't really like living in trailers.' He shivered. 'They're even draughtier than the castle!'

Prudence giggled.

Reaching down, he picked up her hand and fiddled with the ring on her finger. 'I guess, with the pregnancy and everything, you'd like to live near your family?'

Frowning, she nodded slowly. 'Actually, I *am* living with them. They wanted to be there to help me when the baby comes.'

He stared at her anxiously. 'And that's what you still want, is it?'

Smiling weakly, Prudence leant against him and rubbed her cheek against his. 'No. I want to live with my husband. But I *do* want to be near them.' She sighed. 'It's such a shame. The cottage next door came up for sale and that would have been perfect. But it never even went on the open market. Apparently the buyer offered twice the asking price. I'm not sure why…'

Laszlo gazed at her steadily. 'Maybe he liked the location.' His hand tightened around hers and their eyes met.

She stared at him, confused. And then she realised that he was waiting—waiting for her to understand. '*You* bought it?'

He nodded, his face creasing into a smile. 'Yes. I think your neighbour thought I was insane.' He groaned. 'It's probably the first time ever that a

Romany has paid more than the asking price!' His smile tightened. 'But I had to have it. You see, I wasn't sure you'd even speak to me—'

'So you thought you'd stalk me?' Prudence shook off his hand. But her eyes were dancing.

'I thought if I lived next door you wouldn't be able to avoid me,' he said softly. 'Then all I'd have to do was wear down your resistance.'

'Is that right? And how, exactly, were you going to do that?'

She felt her stomach flutter as his eyes narrowed.

'Let me show you,' he murmured, and then he pulled her into his arms and kissed her until, for the third time that afternoon, she thought she'd faint.

* * * * *